STRENGTH OF AN AFRICAN WOMAN

Michael C. Tredway

DORRANCE
PUBLISHING CO
EST. 1920
PITTSBURGH, PENNSYLVANIA 15238

Dorrance Publishing Co
585 Alpha Drive
Suite 103
Pittsburgh, PA 15238
Visit our website at www.dorrancebookstore.com

ISBN: 978-1-6853-7291-0
eISBN: 978-1-6853-7827-1

STRENGTH OF AN AFRICAN WOMAN

Other Books by this Author:

Smile Across East Africa
Cranberry Quill Publishing, 2012

Tales from around the African Campfire
Dorrance Publishing, 2019

DEDICATION

This writing is dedicated to all the strong women of Faith throughout Africa and around the world.

To the African women I have had the blessings from God to meet, know, and be amazed by their physical strength, intelligence, dedication, independence, and innovation.

To African women in remote villages and in cities; women working in the severe heat, trudging miles on muddy roads; working in the fields or hustling on the streets; women striving to find sufficient food and clothes for their children; women struggling to make a life for themselves, sometimes alone, sometimes for their children at home, sometimes for their parents, and sometimes for extended families.

To my wife, a strong African woman; a product of both the African village and the African city. She struggled and survived significant hardships to be the successful woman, loving wife and mother she is today.

To Maureen, Helen, Hiba, Evelyn, Peris, Maggie, Kendi, Ann, and so many others that have worked so hard to be independent and successful in their own ways. Women that have traveled to foreign countries to work tedious and strenuous jobs, selling shoes and other commodities on the streets, or sometimes working as slave laborers for over-demanding men treating women as less than human. Yet, these women have still found success in their respective journeys due to their own abilities, will to push on, and their Faith in God.

And to my mother, Linda Lou Tredway, while not an African woman herself, she found herself on a transcontinental ship, steaming across the Atlantic Ocean alone, with no friends or family on the ship, as a young 18-year-old newlywed, to meet her husband waiting for her on the North African Coast of Libya. In Tripoli, Libya, Linda Lou had to adapt from the small town life in the hills of West Virginia where she was born and raised; and from the comforts and culture of the United States, to this ancient city in North Africa between the Sahara Desert and the Mediterranean Sea. She had to adjust to living in a compound surrounded by Berbers and Arabs, some barely speaking English, most not speaking English at all. Linda soon became pregnant and had a baby; and soon after she delivered another. She raised her two young children in this strange land. After several years and moving back to the US, Linda soon had a third child. Her husband spent significant time deployed away from home in the US Army with several yearlong tours in Vietnam and Korea. Linda took jobs outside the home to help with family finances and provide for her children. I thank her and praise God she influenced her children with strong Christian Faith and respect for God's values; provided us with nutrition and good health, and what we needed to succeed in life.

Praise God for all these women, for giving them the heart and vigor to push on when their strength and hope is diminished, for keeping them safe and giving them His light to follow through the darkness.

FOREWORD

Soul and Jazz singer Nina Simone wrote the song "Four Women" in 1966. The song portrays a strong black woman in each of the four verses. The song identifies the perceptions, stereotypes, and struggles of the black woman in the 1960s. While Simone intended the song to bring the plight of the black woman to the international conscious, many took offense and considered the song racist and the song was actually banned on many broadcast stations. The first verse introduces the listener to "Aunt Sarah," while, perhaps not intended to portray an actual contemporary woman, she is the embodiment of a strong, long-enduring slave woman. This first verse is relevant to not only the honored memory of slaves and traditional black history, but even to the current plight of women in many African cultures: abused and marginalized, yet still strong and proud.

Africa can be a hard and unforgiving place. Many places in Africa, especially in the bush, are isolated worlds filled with darkness, where only the strong can survive. Perception of strength is difficult. What is perceived as the strongest can sometimes be conquered by something not normally considered as strong. A crocodile in the Nile River is one of the fiercest and strongest animals of that realm, but can be easily defeated by a single bite of the hippopotamus. A lion is considered the King of the Jungle in Africa; however, he can be defeated easily by an elephant, a rhinoceros, or a Cape Buffalo, especially a female protecting her young. Life in the darkness is tough and dangerous. People living there have to be tougher.

In most locations in Africa, society and the perception of life is dominated by men. However, it is the women that are the strong backbone of the village and actually run life. A strong woman of Africa allows the perception that men dominate. Generally, women in the African Bush are mostly content in their personal knowledge that they are the gears turning the machine of life.

The men gather beneath the neem tree discussing the trivial matters of life in the village while pretending their pontifications are in the highest and most dire interest of the village. Meanwhile, the women gather the crops, mill the maize, raise the children, and accomplish all the chores required in the village and the home including preparing the meals for the men, making, fixing, and cleaning the men's clothes, and ensuring that their men are prepared for the day. It is a suppressed knowledge that the man would be destitute without the woman.

The women work the fields and harvest the crops.

The women prepare the food.

The women run the markets.

Even in times of conflict, it is the woman that helps the man fight in the bush. And it is the woman who protects the village.

All three previous photos taken of an obelisk statue found in the jungle off a dirt road outside Moamba, Mozambique with paintings depicting the roles of women on three sides.

(Photos by Tredway)

The women bear the children. The women teach the children. The women care for the children and prepare them to be the next generation of life. So, you see, it actually is the woman that runs life.

I used to have pillowcases embroidered by my aunt, given to my wife and me as a wedding gift; one said, "I am the rooster... I rule the roost!" The other one said, "I am that hen... I rule the rooster!"

It is a comfortable symbiotic relationship for the woman to allow the man to think he rules. The man has his ego inflated and struts around as one so important should. But it is the woman that knows she is in true control. It is the internal strength of a woman that is the dominating factor.

One ancient tale from Mozambique emphasizes the strength of the woman.

Many years ago, just outside a remote village deep in the thick bush jungle of Mozambique, there lived a large snake, the largest snake man had ever seen. The men of the village called it Cobra, the Portuguese word for snake, and they were very afraid of "Cobra."

Cobra stayed up in the trees just outside the village, and when the men would leave the village to go hunt or go trade with other villages, Cobra would prepare for his meal. Cobra could not see very good, but he could hear the men approaching and he could feel the body heat as a man passed by underneath. Cobra would drop down just as a man passed by underneath, swallow the man's head, and suck the man up into his large cavernous belly. The other men would run away back to the village and tell the story of the large snake.

The village would try to sustain itself for a week or two, but, as this was the only path in or out of the village, eventually the men would have to go out to hunt and trade with other villages. They would be cautious as they ventured out along the narrow path, but each time, the snake would grab one man for his meal. After a few times, the men of the village knew that they would have to get past the snake to hunt and trade, so they began to devise methods of running past the snake as the Cobra devoured one of their brothers; one after another. It was sad to consider giving up the life of a brother, but it was what they would have to do for the village to survive. So, each time they would go out, they would lose a young man to Cobra. And of course, they had to come back to the village after hunting and trading, so the giant snake would get another meal when they returned, time after time. As weeks went by, so many of the village's young men were eaten by Cobra and Cobra kept getting bigger and stronger.

After some time, there were so few young men left in the village, the village women met around the village campfire and discussed what they could do. If Cobra continued to eat all the young men of the village, there would not be any men left to protect the village; there would not be any men to hunt or trade with the other villages; and of course, there would not be any young men left for the young women to be with.

One young woman, Isabella, tall, lean, and fit, spoke up to the group of women. Isabella told the women that what she had learned from the men coming back from outside the village after Cobra had feasted, it seemed that Cobra would hide in a tree with branches hanging over the path and wait until he felt the heat of a man passing beneath. The women discussed what the men had told them. Cobra could not see very well. Also, Cobra was very slow, because of the way birds and monkeys could sneak up on him and harass him. Cobra, however, was strong and could feel the heat as the men passed beneath the cool tree branches and drop swiftly on the man's head, consuming him. All the women started discussing amongst themselves the shocking details of the men's stories of the strength of Cobra and how Cobra could suck the man up into Cobra's gullet, lifting the man slowly off the ground inch by inch as the man disappeared through the gate of Cobra's fangs. Once the deafening individual discussions of the women had decreased, Isabella began talking again. Isabella told the women that she would go out with the men on the next hunting party with a plan to trick Cobra and kill him. After some more detailed planning and coordinating with the men, who were very reluctant to let a woman protect the village, the next hunting party departed the village with Isabella in the lead. Isabella carried a large kettle of boiling hot water on her head (it was extremely heavy, but common for rural African women to carry heavy things on their head).

Isabella walked very slow but tried not to be suspicious to Cobra as she did not know which tree he might be hiding in. Cobra heard the patrol of seeming village men approaching and began to hang down from his branch. Cobra could feel the heat of the men as they approached.

As Isabella walked beneath the branch Cobra was hanging from, Cobra felt the heat and descended quickly. Cobra's nose hit the water in the steel pot first, and the sensation of the almost still boiling water shocked him. The shock caused all Cobra's muscles to loosen and he lost his grip on the branch. Cobra slid down into the pot of scalding water until his entire length was submerged.

Cobra struggled, but the heat of the water caused his muscles to fail and Cobra drowned. The men continued on their hunt to bring back a Kudu (large antelope) big enough for the entire village to celebrate. Isabella returned to the village with the pot with Cobra inside. The women stoked up the fire and they put the pot in the coals to boil the meat of Cobra thoroughly and they all ate him and buried his bones before the men returned from their hunt. The men did return to the village that evening, safely and with two of the largest Kudu they had ever hunted before. The women prepared the Kudu for the feast and everyone in the village celebrated with dance, song, and fine eating. The men asked about what Isabella had done with Cobra's body? The women just responded that they had buried it. The men designated the site as an honor to Isabella and they later established a monument there.

The Cobra Woman Statue in Maputo, Mozambique honoring
the War Veterans from Mozambique that died in World War I
and World War II. (Photo by Tredway)

It is the strength of the African Woman that is told in this story of a strong woman; a woman that has faced circumstances that could quite possibly crush a man of less faith.

This book tells of the struggles of an African woman. These are stories of her strength, courage, intelligence, and most importantly, her faith in God and the perseverance that faith brought her. We celebrate her, God's Almighty Grace and all the strong African women of faith.

SARAH

My skin is black
My arms are long
My hair is wooly
My back is strong.

Strong enough to take the pain,
Inflicted, again and again.

What do they call me?
My name is Aunt Sarah…
My name is Aunt Sarah…
Aunt Sarah

- Four Women by Nina Simone

This Sarah's skin is not so black, but more a light milk-coffee brown. Her hair is not so wooly but a straight course, dusty, almost rusty brown; she wears it almost shoulder length now, with streaks of dark rusty-orange highlights. As an adult, Sarah is relatively short, muscular and firm, with wide shoulders, a thin waist, sturdy hips, and powerful legs. She has an exceptionally resilient back and is a very strong woman, both physically and mentally. Some of her build is from good Ethiopian/Tigrinya genetics, but comes mostly from the rough young adult life she led and her dedication to stay fit so as to not let anyone abuse her any longer. As a young teenager, Sarah was lean and not so muscular. As she grew into adulthood, both her body and spirit would be toughened by an almost unimaginable tragic life that only her strong faith in God and determined spirit could get her through.

CHAPTER 1

YOUTH AND WAR

Sarah was born in a small village near the town of Dekemhare in northern Ethiopia in 1985. Dekemhare is a small town in the south-central region of what is now the country of Eritrea. Eritrea won its independence from Ethiopia in 1991. By the time of Sarah's birth, northern Ethiopia had already been fighting for its rights as an autonomous country for over 20 years. Dekemhare had been a relatively rich industrial area, established and occupied by the Italians in the 1880's until being defeated by the British in World War II; occupied with attempts at reconstruction by the British from 1941 – 1952; and Ethiopian domination and neglect since then. Under Ethiopian rule, the people of the region felt mistreated and under-represented. A long civil war began and lasted over 30 years. During the civil war, Dekemhare and its industrial complex was destroyed. The area around Dekemhare, and all of what is now Eritrea, is a formidable wasteland, semi-desert—extremely arid, and awfully rocky. The temperatures are some of the highest in the world. The environment does not provide easy living or comfort. It was a difficult life there, especially during a civil war, difficult to eke out a living; difficult to support a family; difficult living conditions; poor education; and inadequate medical facilities. Bringing a baby into this harsh environment would be challenging enough; bringing a new baby, another mouth to feed, another child to clothe and provide medical care for, when your family already has eight children, would seem insurmountable and bring unbelievable stress for the new parents.

Sarah was born as the youngest in a family of nine children. Her father, Isaac, was a very strict and strong man, while her mother, Semhar, was a happy easy-going and loving woman. Sarah's father had been working for a factory in the capital city of Addis Ababa (capital of Ethiopia, far from the civil war) while her mother and older brothers took care of their small home and their animals in the village near Dekemhare. They owned a few cows, some sheep and goats to help them survive. Money from Isaac did not come regularly because of the war, but Semhar used what little she had to run the family. It was always important to Isaac and Semhar that their children attend school. School fees were high, but they used what little they had, even compromising on food and clothing to pay the fees for all the children. The children worked hard in the field with the animal chores and struggled to still make good grades in school in order to reach for a better life. Isaac worked hard for the factory to provide for his family. He was a dedicated man who cherished his family. He also loved his people and the idea of a country free from its southern oppressors.

When Sarah was still very young, Isaac (a Tigray) began to be ostracized and discriminated against by the southern Ethiopians (mostly Amharic) in the factory where he worked. He was eventually forced to leave the factory in the capital city due to the discrimination enraged by the civil war. Isaac managed to migrate back through the civil war lines to the Dekemhare area to be with his family and his people. He sacrificed a lot to work undercover with the revolutionaries fighting the war in remote areas. In between long revolutionary planning sessions and the battles he participated in, Isaac came home to see his wife, Semhar, his seven sons, and his two daughters.

While he loved all his family, Isaac loved his youngest daughter, Sarah, the most. He would always tell Sarah that when the war was over and he was old, he would live with her and rock her children, his precious grandchildren, on his knee. His time with her was always short, as he had to get back for another planning session or another battle. Isaac was captured by the Ethiopians and put in war prison. Isaac suffered extreme torture from the time of his capture in 1989, until his release upon the ceasefire signed in 1991. After his release, Isaac stayed home most of the time, almost completely crippled from the torture. Sarah was six years old then. She remembers her father as a good, loving, dedicated family man, but extremely sad and troubled from the torture. He was devastated that he could not work in the factories any longer to support his family. Isaac spent a lot of time with Sarah and always stressed the importance of her finishing school, finding a good husband, and raising her children with God as their focus. Isaac died in 2005 due to health complications directly related to the conditions of his imprisonment and torture, and perhaps, indirectly, due to the torture of missing and worrying over his baby girl, Sarah. Isaac died before he could ever have the chance of rocking Sarah's son on his knee.

Sarah can still remember the Ethiopian war planes and helicopters flying over her home during the civil war. If Sarah, her sister, or her brothers were in the field with the sheep or goats, and heard the planes coming, they would shout warnings and run to find one of the underground shelters they shared with the rest of the village. Although Sarah did not actually start school until after the war was finished, she remembers her sister and brothers coming home from their school telling their stories of how the planes dropped bombs near the school. The children had to run to the school storage room and pile on top of each other to be protected from the crumbling school being shaken by the bombs. One of Sarah's older brothers died from a bomb attack when he was in the village market.

The bombings became so devastating around Sarah's village the village was destroyed. Sarah's family had to walk for days to another village further north, near the coastal town of Massawa, where her grandmother lived, because the bombings were not as frequent there. Sarah remembers her mother and brothers taking turns carrying Sarah and sometimes her sister Miriam (just two years older than Sarah) on their backs, through the rocky terrain. They had to run for cover several times from the plane bombings and the helicopters shootings. Although Sarah was very young then, and it was so many years ago, Sarah still remembers hearing the gunshots fired from the Ethiopian military helicopters and seeing the victims lying dead. Sometimes, as they were walking to Massawa, Sarah could look down from where she was being carried and remembers her mother's or her brother's legs stepping over the dead bodies. Sarah still has nightmares of this time and is easily frightened by loud noises. As an adult , she has a morbid curiosity about guns. Sarah is still terrified of fireworks during celebrations or even the smallest sound of the crack of a faraway gunshot.

The people of Eritrea finally won their independence from the Ethiopian government after a war of more than two decades that took the lives of hundreds of thousands. Sarah's family moved to Asmara, the capital city of Eritrea, after the end of the war. After being released from the war prison, Sarah's father, Isaac, reunited with his family in Asmara. Isaac could not work in the factories because of his war wounds and treatment from the prison camp, but was able to get a part time job in the market. Sarah's brothers, being much older got jobs too, to support the family. Sarah's mother, Semhar, also had to work outside the home as a cleaning woman. They all worked so the younger children could go to school.

Sarah enjoyed school in Asmara. She had not gone to school in the village during the civil war, but she remembered stories her brothers and sister told her of it being so much different than the schools in the city. In the village, all children sat in the same classroom, regardless of age. The village school was dirty; the teacher seldom showed up for class; the teaching was very disorganized; and of course, the almost daily bombing raids made learning extremely difficult. And there was no recess or free time.

In Asmara, Sarah's school was very organized, at least it seemed so for Sarah. It was much nicer than the school building in the village; it had doors, windows, and many classrooms inside, and there were no bombings to run from. Sarah enjoyed school very much. She was anxious to learn in school and she made good friends. She adapted well to the new life. Sarah had two good friends, Salam and Rahwa. Salam was a very witty girl. She was the oldest in her family, adventurous and fearless. Rahwa, however, was quiet and usually the last one to get persuaded to do new challenges.

The three girls became very good friends and did all kinds of fun things together. Sometime their fun activities got Sarah in trouble with her brothers. Her brothers loved Sarah, but they were over-protective of her and overzealous in their wanting to teach her life lessons. When they caught Sarah doing what they perceived as wrong, they beat her. Her brothers punished Sarah for doing even relatively innocent young girl fun things like looking at dresses in the street stores; playing tag in the market; talking and laughing with boys; and especially for coming home late or dirty. Although Sarah admits that her brothers beat her too hard and too often, she remembers specific things that she still thinks were deserving of her beatings.

When Sarah was 12 years old, she and Salam climbed the wall to residential compound that had a swing. Sarah had seen people swinging before, but had never had the chance; she had wanted to swing so much. Before they dropped down from the wall, they made sure that there was no one in the compound and they snuck over to the swing. Sarah and Salam took turns pushing each other in the swing most of the afternoon. They were having so much fun, they did not notice when the owners came home and caught them. The girls were taken to the police and Sarah's brothers had to come and get her. When Sarah was taken home, her brothers beat her.

Another time, when she was 13 years old, Sarah played a "game" Salam had told her she had tried once. Salam told Sarah she would make her family feel sorry for her if she played the "Run Away Game." Sarah faked running away from home. Sarah left a note that told her family she was hurt, sad, and angry at her brothers, and she had to leave. She snuck out of the house; actually, she told her mother she was going out to get water at the communal spigot. When she got outside, she took off running. Her mother saw her run and called one of Sarah's brothers. Sarah's brother chased her. She ran through the city streets until she lost her brother and she hid in one of the city clothing stores. She hid until just after midnight when she heard the police announcing her name on loud speakers. She looked out the window and she saw her mother and father crying in the street as the police were checking every store. Sarah came out of the store before the police searched it. The police took Sarah and her family to the police station for some questions. Then Sarah went home with her family. She learned that it did not help her family feel sorry for her; it only made her family worry about her, watch her more carefully, and of course it earned Sarah a severe beating when she got home.

Sarah once stole a sheep from a herd. She didn't know what she was going to do with it, perhaps she thought she could kill it and eat it. But she knew she really couldn't kill anything. Maybe she could keep it as a pet, but her family would just make her put it in with their own herd or make her give it back to where she took it from. It was a small sheep and she carried it for as far as she could. When Sarah could not carry the sheep any further, she put the sheep in another field. When she got home, Sarah was so dirty from carrying the sheep and her shirt was torn. She tried to bathe quickly and hide her clothes, but she was caught and beaten.

Sarah was very good with football (soccer) as a teenager. Because in strict Eritrean/Ethiopian Orthodox Church culture, girls were not allowed to play football. Sarah's family was very strict with their religious rules including not allowing Sarah to play sports. Sarah would have to go far outside her neighborhood after school to play in football matches with the boys. She could only manage to go once or twice a week and she tried to hide her football playing clothes, but would still get caught quite often and was beaten each time. Sarah enjoyed the football playing enough to continue the behavior, even considering the beatings she knew she would receive.

Sometimes the beatings were extreme. One time, one of her brothers was beating her while another brother was holding her and they accidentally broke Sarah's arm. Salam and Rahwa tried to help Sarah run away from her brothers a few times, but her brothers always caught her and punished her even more. There is an old traditional belief in Eritrea that if you are scared of getting in trouble put a small rock in your pocket and it will protect you from the wrath. Sarah started carrying a rock in her pocket every day and she prayed to God for protection and for God to guide her every night. She remembers carrying a rock in her pocket every time she went out with her friends, especially to places where she was not supposed to be, on her way home from playing football, or when she thought she would get home past the curfew her brothers had set for her. She did not mean to be a bad girl, and as she grew older and listened to her friends at school talk about their activities, she questioned if she even was a bad girl at all, or if it was just her brothers being overly oppressive.

Sarah's mother, Semhar, loved Sarah despite her rebellious behavior and was good to her. Semhar treated Sarah's wounds after her brothers beat her. Semhar, however, could not stop Sarah's brothers from beating her because in Eritrean culture, a mother doesn't interfere in her grown (post-pubescent) sons' behavior. Sarah's father, Isaac, because he loved Sarah so much, also attempted to comfort her after the beatings, but he was too weak to stop his sons. Although they loved Sarah, appreciated her zest for life, and hated the beatings, Isaac and Semhar agreed with the traditional rules their sons set for Sarah. Sarah continued to follow her friends and exhibit her independent behavior. Sarah's brothers continued the beatings.

CHAPTER 2
CONSCRIPTION AND MARRIAGE

As they became older, reaching the age of 16, Sarah's brothers joined the Eritrean army one by one. The Eritrean law included conscription requiring every youth, male and female, to serve time in the military, mandatory four years for men and mandatory two years for women. All children were required to register for national service when they turned 15 years old and join the Eritrean army on their 16th birthday or at the completion of the second year of high school. The parents could file for an exemption if their child's school marks were in the top of their class and the parents could show financial records proving they had sufficient money for the child to complete the National University; after which, the child would still have to complete four years as a military officer. Girls could also get an exemption if they were married. The army life was difficult and training was brutal for Sarah's brothers, but they adapted and sent what little money they earned home so the younger children could finish their education.

The oldest two brothers were forced to join the Eritrean military. Sarah's third oldest brother joined voluntarily so he could fly helicopters. The rest of her brothers were conscripted in order. Soon after the youngest brother was conscripted, Sarah's sister, Miriam, turned 16 and, because she was not married, she was conscripted into the Eritrean Army for mandatory national service. Although her family was upset that she was going into the army, Miriam was actually very excited about going. Miriam had always been very athletic and very strong. Although she didn't play sports like Sarah did, Miriam was always going out into the field with her brothers to work with the sheep and goats, hiking long distances, and carrying sheep across her shoulders. Miriam was ready for the challenge and did very well in the Army.

Sarah, Salam, and Rahwa finished elementary and junior high school together. After junior high school, before she turned 15 years old, Rahwa's family moved across the southern border to northern Ethiopia for better employment opportunities for her father, and to keep Rahwa from being registered for conscription into the Eritrean military for national service. Sarah and Salam went to high school together and when each girl turned 15 years old, they were required to register for national service.

Sarah's father, Isaac, lost the part time job he had as the health problems from the war prison torture became worse. He was unable to work at all now. Isaac, Semhar, and Sarah had to move to a less expensive neighborhood in Asmara. When they moved, Isaac thought it was a good time for Sarah to stop school as no one in the new neighborhood would know Sarah, or her age, and it would be easier for her to hide from the National Service Investigators. Sarah started working in a small street store in the city. Between her job and trying to keep a low profile, she was not able to see her friends as often she wished. Sarah still visited Salam when she could. Sarah and Salam both missed Rahwa very much and would talk about all the fun they used to have together.

There were many stories of how young girls were treated in the army. Even Sarah's sister Miriam had been abused in the army several times when she first joined. Isaac did not want his youngest daughter to go through this torture. Sarah did not want to join the military either. It wasn't the abuse that concerned Sarah the most, as she had been beaten by her brothers most of her life; it was the thought of killing that bothered her. Sarah had begun going to an underground evangelical church at night. Only the Ethiopian Orthodox Church was legal in Eritrea. Sarah's new church taught of a more loving God and taught of loving each other more intense than the church Sarah grew up in. The doctrine of the new church was strictly against the fighting and killing, and the military in general. Sarah's brothers had also told Army stories of drinking alcohol, chewing Khat (a leafy drug Eritreans chew to get high), having wild parties and how the male soldiers used the female soldiers for free sex. Sarah knew she could not survive spiritually if she joined the army. Sarah and Isaac would talk for hours of how terrible it would be if Sarah joined the military and they worked to devise plans to keep her safe from the conscription.

Sarah had to stop working at the dress shop in town in order to keep a lower profile. Sarah stayed at home unemployed for a few weeks, but knew she needed to help her mother and father financially. It was hard seeing how her family struggled to where most days they only had a few wraps of injera (the main staple of Ethiopia and Eritrea; a sour flat bread) to eat for dinner and dinner was the only meal of the day. And it was really difficult for her to stay cooped up in her room all day, every day. Sarah began working part time in an oil refinery. Because she had not finished school and had not completed her national service, Sarah had to work illegally and was not paid good wages, but it was enough to help. When she was not working, she had to hide on the streets and from the neighbors so they would not report her.

Isaac and Sarah knew they needed a more permanent and sustainable solution to keeping her from national service. Sarah did not have the education background and grades required to go straight into University and avoid the conscription. The only solution they could think of was for Sarah to get married. If she were married, she would be disqualified for initial entry in to the Eritrean military. Sarah would be allowed to go to University and have the education Isaac dreamed for his children, which was especially important for Isaac since none of his other children had escaped the compulsory national service or gone to University. Sarah did not have a boyfriend and was not interested in anyone to marry. However, when Sarah was born, there was a close family with a son, Yonis, whose parents had agreed with Isaac and Semhar to marry Yonis and Sarah as soon as they were of age. This was a matter of tradition and not binding, even mostly forgotten. It was only now, in this dire situation, that Semhar and Isaac remembered it. They were not sure if Yonis was still unmarried. Yonis was two years older than Sarah, that would make him 19 years old now and probably still in the Eritrean military. They had not seen or talked to Yonis' family since Sarah's family had left the village near De-kemhare. Isaac and Semhar called family and friends from the old village for two days until Semhar was finally able to talk with Yonis' mother. Yonis' father had died, but his mother still remembered Semhar and Sarah and their traditional marriage agreement. And Yonis was still unmarried.

At the risk of Sarah's evasion from national service being discovered, Semhar told her old friend the story of Sarah and their idea for Sarah to marry Yonis. Semhar proposed that it would just be a temporary marriage; they could divorce after two years if they were unhappy. Yonis' mother said she would talk the proposal over with Yonis and the elders of the family. Semhar pled with her to be discrete so as not to alert National Security Services. Two days later, Semhar received a return call that Yonis was considering the proposal and would decide after talking to Sarah. Yonis called Sarah and they spoke together for several hours. Yonis was attending University in Massawa near the coast. He would come to Asmara and stay with Sarah's family for one week to plan the wedding; Sarah and Yonis would get married. Yonis would return to Massawa after the wedding, while Sarah would stay in Asmara with Isaac and Semhar.

During the week leading up to the marriage, Sarah and Yonis talked a lot. They agreed that they would not sleep together until at least after Sarah's 18th birthday as she was just 17 years old at the time of the wedding. Yonis could tell that Sarah was nervous as he sat next to her. Yes, Sarah was very nervous, even frightened to be married to a man that she was just meeting for the first time. But they talked easily together. Sarah appreciated Yonis' understanding of her situation. Yonis was patient, sensitive, and educated. She still could not help but tremble when she sat next to him. Yonis stayed in Isaac's and Semhar's house, but he slept on the kitchen floor and never entered Sarah's room. He would walk Sarah to her work and meet her there to walk her home. It was important for people to see them together before the wedding. The wedding was small with only a few neighbors invited, just enough to make it look real so the neighbors could convince the national investigators when they asked questions about Sarah.

Yonis went back to Massawa the day after the wedding to continue his schooling. Sarah stayed with her parents. It was a very plausible story and no one questioned the situation. Sarah no longer had to hide and felt more secure walking in town. She could go shopping. Sarah talked to her supervisor at the oil refinery and was able to become a legitimate employee. Her new status at work provided her considerably more income. She was able to contribute more to her parent's finances and save some money for herself for when if the façade ended and she would have to run from the government.

Yonis was a good man. He studied hard and succeeded in his studies at University. He stayed faithful to his marriage vows, even though he knew it was without love. Yonis stayed in Massawa and Sarah stayed in Asmara. They never saw each other again after the wedding.

Sarah began planning her 18th birthday party. The past year had been good for her. She had a good job, earned good money, had made friends at work and at a couple of the clothing stores and markets in town, and had almost forgotten her life in hiding. She invited her new friends to the party. Her birthday celebration was not so big, but it was enough to attract attention.

Talk from the neighbors reached Semhar's ears that governmental investigators were asking questions about Sarah and her husband. The neighbors had not seen Yonis in over a year, not since the wedding. National Service Investigators came around all the time asking about everyone's teenage children. Maybe one of the neighbors mentioned Sarah and her lonely marriage. Or, perhaps she was reported by one of her work colleagues that she may have accidentally joked with about her "Fake Marriage" when conversations were raised about Sarah's husband never being with her. He didn't even come to her 18th birthday party. Semhar, Isaac, and Sarah talked about the gossip, the potential problems, and began planning again. Even though Sarah was married and officially exempt from joining the military, because she did not have children, they might be able to take her away and make her join anyway.

Yonis started calling Sarah on her cell phone soon after their one-year wedding anniversary. He was becoming unhappy with the situation. He was getting close to graduation. Yonis was considering his life after graduation, a real marriage, children. He had met a girl that he would like to be with and told Sarah he was considering filing for divorce. Sarah begged Yonis to wait until after his graduation to file for divorce because without children and without even a husband, she would have to go into hiding again. Three months after Sarah's 18th birthday, just a month after their one-year wedding anniversary, Yonis called to tell Sarah he had filed for divorce.

Semhar continued to get information from some of the neighbors closest to her that the government informants were asking more questions about Sarah and her husband. Sarah knew that it would only be a short time before the divorce papers reached the National Service Office in Asmara from Massawa where Yonis filed.

There were new border conflicts between Ethiopia and Eritrea with several small armed battles. One of Sarah's brothers died in one of them. This was the second son of Isaac and Semhar to die because of the conflict. It hit Sarah really hard when her second brother died. She was also concerned for her other brothers and her sister that were on the front lines of the conflict. Along with the spiking battles, the need for recruitment was increased and National Service Investigators were becoming even more active.

Sarah had stopped going to the underground evangelical church she had been attending after she heard that she was a person of interest in the National Service Investigations. But now, with renewed concerns of being caught and the recent death of her brother, Sarah needed renewed strength in God. She found and started attending underground Bible studies in secret houses of believers. Even with her early background in the Ethiopian Orthodox Church and the time she spent at the underground Evangelical Church, she did not know much about the word of God or a life as a "Born Again." In these Bible studies, she found new friends and the best friend of all; she found a true spiritual friendship in Christ. Sarah felt a new kind of faith inside her that she never felt before. She started reading the Bible and getting comfort from it. She found that Christ had a special and meaningful life ahead for her and Jesus would be with her no matter what happened. Sarah remembers the day the soldiers came to the home where they were having the Bible study after a neighbor reported their loud nightly singing and praising. She almost got caught then, but she is sure that it was Jesus that helped her get away.

CHAPTER 3

RUNNING AWAY

With her new faith, Sarah began to see how the devil was attacking her with all his power. Isaac and Semhar were not happy with her going to the Bible studies. Sarah tried to talk to them about her new faith and how wonderfully amazing the comfort of Jesus Christ was, but they were too set in their comfortable traditional Orthodox Christianity. Isaac and Semhar, as most Eritreans, were proud of their religion and their rituals. They were descendants of the Queen of Sheba and King Solomon, the son of King David of Israel. They were hurt that their baby daughter, who they had been risking everything for, would turn her back on their icons, traditions, and ancestors. As much as they loved Sarah and wanted to protect her, with her breaking away from the Orthodox Church, and with the National Service Investigators getting closer, they agreed it was time for Sarah to leave their home.

Sarah was 18 years old, out on her own but not alone. She knew Jesus was with her and had faith He would protect her and giver her strength. Sarah started moving from one relative to another, and to friends she had met at the Bible studies, asking for shelter. She could only stay at each place for a few days at a time because the investigators were becoming more active. The organizers of the Bible study group helped Sarah a lot and organized a plan for her to move with other girls to Adi Keyh in southeastern Eritrea, south of Dekemhare. Then the girls could cross to Ethiopia or continue south to Assab, in the southern Eritrean panhandle, and move on to Djibouti.

The members of the Bible study group had helped others escape Eritrea and were willing to help Sarah. Sarah had a little money of her own, but they gave her the extra money she would need to pay the people to transport her, hide her, and help her illegally cross the border. Sarah was ready to begin the journey. She would travel with four other people and a guide arranged and paid for by the Bible study group. They travelled at night to avoid the soldiers and investigators.

Everyone in their small group was scared and excited. All five of the runners had mostly grown up in Asmara and had never seen wild animals like the hyenas they found themselves surrounded by, eyes glowing and snarling at them when they were walking at night. The Bible study group had arranged some vehicle transportation, pick-ups at designated spots on the outside of small towns and drop-offs a few miles down the road, but mostly the group walked. The trails were uneven and rough, rocky and dry. They travelled at night and hid during the day. They ran out of their food and water after three nights. They were past contact with the Bible study group now. They could not go into the villages to buy food because government informants were everywhere and would turn them in. Sarah remembers being so hungry, she and another girl ate the coconut skin lotion she had in her bag.

The trip was taking longer than the Bible group had planned. The person the group paid to lead them to Adi Keyh left them alone on the fourth day. He told them to stay at their camp until he returned with more money, food, and help. They feared the possibility of the man returning with government agents or soldiers and collecting a reward for turning them in. They discussed if they should wait or the alternative of pushing on without him and trying to cross the border on their own. They were frightened by both options and argued. The two men of the group of five decided to move out on their own as they suspected their guide might hand them over. The three ladies, including Sarah, decided to wait for the guide to find them in their hiding place. After two days, the guide returned empty handed, no food or water. He told the girls that he was also in hiding as the soldiers were all around and actively searching for army deserters.

Sarah cried and prayed hard. The guide, Sarah, and the other two girls left their hiding spot about an hour before sundown and started walking. They were so hungry and thirsty. Sarah remembers thinking it was strange, though, it seemed the hunger pains were decreasing, but she was getting more tired, easier. Each step took so much effort and energy. One of the other girls kept falling and could not walk on her own. They took turns helping her. Their movement was so slow. They continued, only moving during the nights and resting during the days.

On the third day after the guide returned (the ninth day after leaving Asmara), while all three girls were sleeping, Sarah was laying on her side. She felt the guide creep up behind her and hold her close with one hand over her mouth. He worked to lift her shirt and pull down her pants. Sarah was too exhausted to fight, but she squirmed as much as she could to make it more difficult for him. With her skin exposed, she could feel he was naked. Sarah could feel him try to enter her from behind. She squirmed as hard as she could and was able to free her arm. She turned as much as she could to hit him and push him off her. She poked him in the eye and he ran away. Sarah woke the other two girls and they sat up together forming a triangle so they could guard themselves in all directions in case he returned. As they sat there, whispering to each other, one of the other girls broke down crying. The guide had raped her the day before;, this girl had been too weak to fight him and too ashamed to say anything until then. The guide did not return.

The girls waited two hours and started walking. It was almost dark when they began and the girls walked through the night. They moved so slow; they were weak and tired. They knew they were close to the Ethiopian border now. They found and paralleled a small road they thought would lead them to the border, but did not go so close to be visible to people on the road. Just after sunrise, as they were just sitting down to rest, they saw a family of nomads moving their herd of cattle. Sarah walked ahead to the road leaving the other two girls behind in case the nomads became violent. She walked next to and talked to one of the women, an old woman.

Sarah told the old woman that her and her friends had been travelling to see relatives in Ethiopia but they had been robbed of their identification and travel permits. It was dangerous exposing themselves to strangers, but they had to trust someone and they needed help to get across the border. The woman seemed receptive and went to tell one of the men. Sarah went back and got the other two girls. The nomads accepted the girls into their group. They told the girls it was still a two-day walk to the border at the slow pace they were using to push the cattle. The men told the girls they were welcome to travel with them as part of their family. They gave the girls water, milk from the cows, and injera to eat. They ate so much, one of the girls vomited but was laughing… they all laughed, even the nomad men were laughing hard. After eating, the family packed up and continued to move during the day. Sarah and the other two girls were allowed to ride on the old bulls of the herd. After several hours, the group stopped to rest and let the cattle graze. The nomads set up tents and put the girls in the tent with the other young girls and children. Sarah and the other two girls felt safe. They had full stomachs and slept well, better than they had since they had started the journey over ten days ago. They slept comfortably through the heat of the late afternoon and through the cool night. The girls were awakened in the morning by soldiers shaking them with their feet and putting the barrels of their AK 47 rifles in the girls' faces.

The nomads had turned the girls in to the Eritrean authorities. The nomads were not intentionally bad people; they had to work and cooperate with government officials in order to travel freely on the road and protect their cattle. The men of the nomad group did not believe the girls' story of visiting relatives, three young girls would not be travelling so far alone to visit relatives.

CHAPTER 4

CAPTURED

When they were captured, the girls were actually only a few kilometers from the Ethiopian border. The road they had been paralleling was relatively un-protected by border patrols on either side. Left alone, the girls may have been able to cross the border and been free in Ethiopia. Both sides of the border in that area, especially along the road, however, were crowded with hidden anti-personnel landmines. If they had continued on their own, they would most likely have been killed. Sometimes, God works miracles we don't realize.

The girls were taken to the town of Renda, near the Ethiopian Border, near the Denakil Province boundary of the Eritrean southern panhandle. They were held in a small police jail cell for two days. National Service Investigators came from Asmara to interrogate the girls. The girls stayed to the story that they went walking to look for gold in the mountains and they got lost, the story the Bible study group had told them to rehearse.. They said over and over again that they were not planning on crossing the border. If they con-fessed to that, they would have been shot immediately for treason. On the third day, the girls were tied with ropes and forced to walk behind a slow truck from one village to the next for two days until they reached the city of Adi Keyh. They were given water to drink at each village but only given a small piece of injera at the end of each day when they stopped. They were kept tied but allowed to sleep on the ground behind the truck at night.

In Adi Keyh, they were held individually in jail cells alone and interrogated separately. The interrogations were more sophisticated and the beatings were worse. While on the way to Adi Keyh, the beatings were just slaps across the face and fists in the stomach. In Adi Keyh, their shirts were removed with their hands tied high up above their heads and they were whipped across the back and were subjected to humiliations no woman would want to experience. Sarah would close her eyes during the beatings and think about the beatings her brother gave her when she was younger. She would think about the fun things she, Salam, and Rahwa had done. She would imagine swinging in the forbidden swing. Sarah held onto their story for the first day in Adi Keyh. She didn't know what the other two girls were saying. The second day, Sarah was sure the other girls had broken down and had told the truth because the questions they were asking her were more detailed. The investigators broke Sarah, too. She told them she was running, but not the full truth. Sarah said she had run from her home in Dekemhare and met the two other girls in the bush. She told the investigators that she was only 15 years old, not 18, and she was just trying to get away before she was conscripted. None of the girls knew much about the identity of the guide or the people they were supposed to meet at the border. The National Service Investigators kept trying to get answers about the plan from the girls for several more days.

After the second night in Adi Keyh, the girls were only interrogated for a few hours each morning, then they were taken out and locked in a steel shipping container during the rest of the day and through the night. There were five other women already in the shipping container. The smell and the heat inside were beyond comprehension. The steel box was in the middle of a rocky desert in one of the hottest places on earth. The smell was from five sweaty, bloody, dying women, women that had been urinating and defecating in the corners of the container for days, weeks, maybe even months. There were a few holes in the top of each of the four walls of the box. The holes provided sufficient air to breathe, barely, but they failed to provide any circulation of the air. It was dark in the container, Sarah could see the bodies of the five women, but couldn't tell if they were moving or even alive. One of the girls that came in with Sarah began vomiting and that made the smell even worse. The heat and the smell caused Sarah's head to pound. The pain in her head was worse than the pain from the beatings because Sarah couldn't think of her family, her friends, or memories; she could only think of the pain in her head. Sarah would cry and eventually, mercifully, pass out. She would wake up in the mornings because rats would nip on her arms. She saw rats gnawing on the other women that were either too weak to chase them off or already dead.

Sarah doesn't know how long she stayed in the container or how many days of beatings she received. She only knows one day, one of her travelling companions did not return from the interrogations. The next day, Sarah was put into a truck and driven away. She was so weak and wounded; her back and breasts had open wounds from the whippings; her legs and arms were grotesquely swollen; she was bloody everywhere; and her head still hurt more than anything imaginable. She thought maybe she was dead and this was Hell; perhaps she was paying for the wild ways of her youth and sinning against her parents and her brothers. As she felt the truck lunge forward, Sarah passed out.

Prison guards woke Sarah up when they arrived at the Central Prison in Asmara. She was taken to the prison clinic where they treated her wounds. They put her in a cell. They brought her food and water. Sarah was thankful to be out of the shipping container. She said a prayer of thanks to God before she ate.

Sarah stayed in the Asmara prison for two months. They treated her wounds. They treated wounds she didn't know she had, because of the shock and trauma of the abuse in Adi Keyh; one of her legs had been broken and she had several cracked ribs; they splinted Sarah's leg and bandaged her ribs. As time in the Asmara prison continued, they treated Sarah with humane care. Her wounds began to mend. The gashes on her back and breasts healed over and she began to get her strength back. Even though she was in prison, Sarah felt safe and strangely comfortable. She found stability in the daily routine and the exercise the prison physical rehabilitation program allowed her. At the end of the second month, they transferred Sarah to the National Service Office in Dekemhare and processed her for induction into the Eritrean Army.

Sarah liked being in Dekemhare. Seeing her hometown brought back memories of her early childhood and her family being together. She cherished the blue wide-open skies. The sights, the smells, and the knowledge she was near her old home all brought back her fond toddler years. Even though she was not allowed freedom to walk around the town or to go her old village, it still felt like home. The administrative activities only took a few hours each day; the rest of the time each day was spent reading and talking with other female recruits. Sarah made a few friends. All the conscripts were held in tight lock-down, but not punished or treated poorly. After a few days at the Dekemhare military induction center, Sarah began to wonder if her army service would really be all that bad. Maybe two years would pass quickly, she could find a good man, get married, and be released to live a good life.

At the end of the week of in-processing the military at Dekemhare, Sarah was prepared, administratively, but not mentally, to go to the indoctrination and basic training facility for the Eritrean military near Barentu. Sarah and the friends she had made at Dekemhare were frightened of going to Barentu. They had all heard stories from friends and relatives of the abuses of trainees at Barentu. All Sarah could do was pray. Sarah prayed hard.

CHAPTER 5

BARENTU

Barentu is in the middle of the south-central western region of Gash-Barka. Like most of Eritrea, Barentu is rocky desert, extremely hot, and barren. The Eritrean Army Training Center near Barentu was established as the Primary Indoctrination and Initial Training Base because of its isolation from any high concentration of population and the surrounding steep, barren, arid, mountains, making any desertion or escape by the trainees unlikely.

Straight-line distance from Dekemhare to Barentu is actually only less than 100 miles. However, by road, some paved and some not, the route goes northwest through Asmara, continuing northwest to Eritrea's third biggest city, Keren, then southwest to Barentu, traversing over 200 miles. Considering the poor road conditions, the trip required two days including an overnight stop in Keren.

Sarah was forced to sit in the back of a two and a half ton cargo truck, crammed with 27 other female conscripts and two male armed guards. It was tight, elbow to elbow and hip to hip sitting on the bare metal floor of the truck bed. The inductees were dressed in plain khaki uniforms, which would help protect them from the dust and sun; however they were denied footwear (not allowed to have either shoes or socks) to aid in preventing them from escaping. The guards stood up at the front of the truck bed, holding on to the cab, but watching the girls so none of them would jump out of the truck. Even the paved roads were rough and bouncy with potholes and speed bumps in the small towns and villages. But the unpaved roads were even worse, extremely bumpy and so hard on the backsides of the future army trainees. Each bump impacted each girl's tailbone and the pain ran up their spine. Some of the girls were able to position their feet under them to act as cushions, but that only provided them comfort over a few bumps as it would almost dislocate their ankles and twist their knees. As the trip pressed on, the pain became greater and greater.

The truck pulled off the side of the road just a few kilometers before the city of Keren. They were a little over halfway to Barentu and it was getting dark. They had been on a dirt road, but it was wide. The driver turned onto a small trail and the bumps were worse. Most of the inductees were crying and in horrific pain. The truck stopped in front of a few military style tents. They were stopping for the night. The girls were glad when the truck stopped, as much for the ceasing of the bumps as for the chance they would be allowed to stand, stretch their legs, get out of the truck, and go to the bathroom. Many of the girls strained to stand up and some of the female recruits, including Sarah, began to sing praises to God. The guards standing near the cab in the bed of the truck with the girls yelled at the girls and told them to sit down, but most of them stayed standing. With so many bodies, and as tight as the muscles in their legs were, it would have been difficult to sit back down anyway. One of the men sitting in the cab of the truck got out and went into one of the tents. He was in the tent for a few minutes and the girls could hear talking. Then he came back out laughing, running for the truck and screaming at the girls to sit down. He got back into the cab and the truck started back up. The girls were trying to sit down, but the truck started moving too fast and shook the girls. One of the girls fell out of the truck. She screamed loud, then was silent, just lying on the ground like she was dead. The truck kept going. Sarah saw a man come out from one of the tents and drag the girl into the tent.

The truck went back to the main road and continued toward the town of Keren. Those girls still standing struggled to hang on and not fall out. And those sitting or squatting on the floor of the truck bed cried in pain as the road bumps pounded through their legs and backs. The guards continued to tell the girls to sit down a few times, but they were not so forceful, and actually laughed a bit. The truck entered the town and went to a fuel station. While the truck was being filled with fuel, the soldiers from the cab went to a market kiosk to buy food, snacks, and sodas. One of the guards in the truck bed with the recruits jumped out and ran over to the kiosk too. Sarah even saw one of the soldiers buying a bag of Khat (the leafy narcotic drug) to be shared by the soldiers to chew later. The other guard stayed in the truck and yelled at the girls to stay in the truck and sit down. But he was smiling and almost laughing as he anticipated the snacks, the soda, and the Khat. The recruits paid no attention to the guard's half-hearted orders to stay seated. Most of the girls, including Sarah, stood up in the truck.

The soldiers drove the female recruits back to the tents off the main road, after the truck was refueled. Most of the recruits stood in the back of the truck, holding on tight to each other, during this short drive. All the girls were in extreme agony and praying for the day to be over. When the truck arrived back at the tents, two of the soldiers went in to one of the tents while the other three soldiers helped the girls get out of the truck, kept them in a tight group, and guarded them. The other two guards returned from the tent carrying a large wooden crate of handcuffs and chains. One soldier formed a circle with the chains, locking them together and locking the chain circle to the towing pintle hitch of the truck. Two of the soldiers continued to guard the females, with their guns raised and ready in case any of the girls started running away. The last two soldiers from the truck, with two others soldiers from inside the tent, handcuffed all 27 remaining recruits to the chain. The girl that had fallen out of the truck was dragged out of the tent and handcuffed to the chain, too. She was alive, but still unconscious.

The guards brought the conscripts food and water. The food was just several large wraps of injera. The girls shared the injera and passed the bottles of water around. The guards took turns taking the girls to an area about 50 meters behind the tents to relieve their bladders. Some of the recruits had diarrhea, but not many, and those that did have it did not go much as their stomachs had been empty and they were dehydrated. There were not any bathrooms, so it was just a slit trench. As Sarah approached the site where they took her to go, she could smell it. The raucous odor almost made her vomit, but she kept it down.

Except for the unconscious recruit, all of the other female conscripts were taken to void themselves, two at a time, and locked back up to the chain when they returned. One soldier stood guard for a couple hours at a time, then was relieved by another soldier. Sarah thought it was uncomfortable to sleep chained up, but it felt good to be able to stretch out. Sarah slept. She woke up during the night. It was too dark to see at first, until her eyes adjusted; the candles in the tents had been extinguished. There was no ground light; no nearby villages and the town of Karen was still too far away with many tall hills in between. After a minute, the moonlight provided enough light for Sarah to see her immediate surroundings. She could see some of the girls sleeping, while others were sitting, or lying on their side, awake. The soldier on duty guarding the recruits was lying down, not moving, and seemed to be asleep. Sarah thought about her situation and became very frightened. She worried if she would be strong enough to make it the next two years. She began to pray. Sarah asked God for help; then she asked for courage; then she remembered the 23rd Psalm…. "Even though I walk through the valley of darkness, I will fear no evil, for God is with me!" She meditated on this for a few minutes… She looked up and saw the moon. It was full and bright. She could imagine God's face looking down at her, crying for her. God would protect her. It was quiet. There was a cool breeze kissing her face. She thanked God that her wounds had healed and she was healthy. Sarah fell back asleep, comforted by her faith.

When Sarah awoke, the sun was up and the heat had already started to build. Some of the recruits were sitting, some were lying on their sides, while others were still asleep on their stomachs. Sarah could only see one of the females lying on her back; it was the girl that had fallen out of the truck. Was she still unconscious? Sarah didn't know, but she said a prayer for her.

The guards were up and moving around. Two of the guards were kneeling over a fire and appeared to be cooking coffee. One of the guards brought a bag out of the tent. He took injera out of the bag and began passing pieces to the girls. Another soldier brought a jerry can of water and a glass out of the tent. He went to each recruit and poured a cup of water for each, one at a time, as they ate their injera. All the conscripts were awakened as the injera was passed around and the water came, except the one lying on her back. When the soldier with the water got to her, she wouldn't wake. He called out and a sergeant came over. The sergeant checked her breathing and then her pulse. He announced she was dead and called for help. The other guards came, unchained the young recruit, and carried her to the tent. Some of the girls cried. The guards yelled at the recruits to be quiet.

The guards began to unchain the conscripts and escort the females, two at a time, to the slit trench latrine behind the tents. When each pair of females had finished, they were escorted back and loaded onto the truck. After each of the 27 conscripts were in the bed of the truck, the journey to Barentu Indoctrination and Basic Training Facility continued.

The female recruits had not recovered from the previous day's painful ride, and the beginning of this leg of the trip was not any less excruciating.

The girls wanted to stand, but the guards riding in the back with them made the conscripts sit down. The truck moved fast on the road leading into the town of Keren making the bumps in the road hurt worse. As the truck drove through town, however, it slowed and the bumps were not so hurtful. Upon leaving the town of Keren behind them, the truck went faster and the agony of the expedition continued.

The truck drove straight through Keren without stopping and proceeded on west to Barentu. This day's trip was just as uncomfortable and as throbbingly painful as the previous day. The sun scorched down on the young women. The reflected heat from the metal on the truck they were sitting in and the desert rocks they were riding through made it twice as hot. The bumps radiating up through the recruits' ankles and legs agitated up through their already tender backs. With extremely limited space to shift their body positions, the conscripts' legs tensed up again, even quicker and more achingly than the previous day. The dust rising up from the rocky desert road seemed worse this day too. The dust was so thick. It stuck to Sarah's sweaty face and arms. She could feel it adhering to her body everywhere beneath her clothes too. The dust got into Sarah's mouth making it difficult to breathe. Sarah's head began to pound before noon and the day's excursion was not even half finished. Sarah thought it was the longest days of her life. After several more hours, with the pain in her head pounding and severe aches all through her body, Sarah passed out.

It was early evening when the truck finally arrived in Barentu. Sarah was awakened by the other girls' movements. They were all straining to stand up. Sarah felt the cool evening desert air around her as space opened with the recruits getting off the truck. She could hear the guards shouting and some of the female conscripts crying as they were pushed to the ground. The new trainees were forced to lay face down on the rocky desert ground until the Barentu Army Training Center Senior Officer and Commander came out to greet them. The officer, an Army Captain, told the guards to let the women stand up so he could talk to them. Once all the recruits were standing, the Commander began to speak. Sarah doesn't remember much of what he said, perhaps she couldn't hear him as the roaring of the truck tires bouncing on the bumpy road still played in her head. The last of the day's light was grey and dusky and Sarah remembers she could not see the Commander very clearly. She doesn't remember the details of his face from that time when he was giving his indoctrination speech, but she does remember him very clearly from the next time she saw him. She did remember that he was a small man, smaller than the guards standing around him, and even smaller than Sarah herself. Sarah remembers thinking, if not for the guards surrounding the Commander, she could have pushed him down and ran. But the guards around him would stop her before she went very far. Sarah resigned to wait it out a bit and see what the next few days would bring. All she really wanted to do now was to eat and sleep.

After the Commander finished talking to the female conscripts, the guards led the recruits to a large concrete pad with a tin roof and a few lights. The women were instructed to sit down. The guards brought the recruits several rolls of injera and gave each a metal bowl of water. They were told to keep the metal bowl safe as it would be the only one they would get.

After approximately one hour, they had all finished eating and some of the girls were starting to sleep. The guards approached from each corner of the concrete pad and began spraying the recruits with water from large fire hoses. Most of the spray was just over the heads of the conscripts, but sometimes the direct stream would find a target. Sarah remembered how it stung her arms. The water was cold. It soaked Sarah's clothes to her skin. She could feel the cool night air against her wet skin, which made it even colder. But it was nice feeling the dust from the road rinse off her body. Sarah could feel her body breathe as her pores were free from the dried sweat and dirt. The soldiers kept spraying for 15 to 20 minutes, ensuring all the female conscripts were soaked. They stopped spraying the water and told the women to remove their clothing. Some of the recruits began undressing immediately, while other hesitated. Those that were slow to undress were hit by another direct blast of water causing the recipient to scream out in pain from the shock of the cold stinging water. Sarah was somewhere in the middle of the concrete pad surrounded by the other girls. She undressed immediately after seeing the first recruit get a direct water blast because she did not want to get hit by the hose stream and none of the male guards were so close to her that they could see her clearly. After she took her clothes off, Sarah used them to cover her front as best she could. When all the recruits were undressed, the guards began spraying the water on the tops of the conscripts' heads, wetting them completely again. The guards screamed loudly to the recruits to hold their clothes up to ensure that they were washed by the streams of water. The water was sprayed long enough for the women to soak their clothes, wring them out and soak them several times. Long enough for the sweat and the dirt from the long drive to be wrung out of the clothing and off the recruit's bodies.

Sarah was shivering, after being so hot during the truck ride through the desert, and now being doused with the cold water. She was glad when the soldiers stopped the spraying and appeared to be putting the hoses away. Sarah used her wet, but wrung out, clothes to wipe the excess water off her skin. The soldiers started throwing wool blankets out to the females yelling that three girls would share one blanket, to dry off and then to sleep on. The guards ordered the girls to dry as fast as possible and to lie down on the blankets. After all the women were lying down, the soldiers began walking through the mass of bodies sprawled out on the concrete pad shaking delousing powder on the recruits. The soldiers took the women's clothes from them. The conscripts were told to get comfortable as they would be sleeping there for the night. All the recruits, in groups of three, huddled close together trying to warm themselves with their shared wool blankets. Sarah and the two other girls sharing the blanket with her came close together. They lie close to each other. Like a single unit, the girls' bodies were warm. As long as the three girls of each group stayed close together, the wool blanket was big enough for all three girls to lie on with enough left to fold over and cover them. Sarah was thankful to be in the middle as the three girls held each other like sisters sharing a bed. Sarah felt clean, a bit warmer, and somehow safe for the moment.

The conscripts were told not to worry: assured that guards were posted on the outside of the shelter to protect the women from hyenas. Sarah started to sleep, but remembers thinking as she drifted off that the guards were not really there to protect the women from the hyenas, but rather to keep the conscripts from escaping.

Sarah woke up in the early morning sandwiched between the two other girls, feeling very odd from that, but also strangely warm. The sun was just rising and she suddenly felt a cold desert night breeze on her face. Sarah thought she should feel much colder than she was, after being exposed to the cold desert air all night. Then she felt another breeze, but this one was warm. Sarah looked up from between the two other conscripts and saw that there were heater fans mounted on the shelter supports blowing warm air around. She bowed her head, closed her eyes, and gave God praise for the warmth.

While Sarah prayed, the sun rose. As she lifted her head up, she rose up a bit more onto her hands and knees. She could see the sunrise just over the sleeping bodies of the other female conscripts. Sarah saw God's majesty in the sunrise and felt his promise of better days to come. The guards began yelling to wake the recruits up. The soldiers made the women stand up and threw them khaki uniform shorts and t-shirts to put on. They brought them more injera to eat and passed water jugs for the conscripts to pour water into their metal bowls from the previous night.

While the recruits were eating, the soldiers began taking the women, two at a time, to the latrine, a small mud-clay building with a tin roof. Actually, there were two of these small buildings, similar in size and construction, except one had a sign that said "Trainees" and the other had a sign that said "Cadre Only." The "Cadre" latrine had a wooden door and open windows on each of its four walls. The "Trainees" latrine, to be used by the recruits, had no windows, only an open doorway with no door.

As Sarah ate and drank her water, she watched the other girls escorted to the latrine. As the recruits returned, some would whisper to each other of their relief. Sarah began to feel a sudden intense pressure to relieve herself. The combination of sleeping on the cold concrete slab, the cool night air, the long cold dowsing of the water shower, the drinking of the water, and now knowing the other girls were going to the latrine made her pressure almost unbearable. Actually, she was not sure if she might have urinated during the hosing down the night before, but if she did, it wasn't enough because there was so much pressure now. Finally, it was her turn to go. The "Trainee" latrine was dark and smelled inside. She could barely see just a slit trench along one of the walls to squat over. Simple as it was, it was enough. Sarah was so relieved!

It seemed like only a very short time after she returned from the latrine, as the other conscripts finished savoring the injera, satisfying their hunger, all the females had been escorted to the latrine to relieve themselves. The soldiers ordered the conscripts to pick up their metal bowls, leave the blankets on the ground, and form two lines. The guards moved the two rows of conscripts to two long mud-clay buildings with tin roofs where the females would sleep.

Camp located outside Barentu, Eritrea (Photo by Tredway)

As they were moving across the rocky field to the sleeping barracks, Sarah could see other buildings. She would soon learn the utility of each. There was the command office building of relatively good wooden construction, two other mud-clay buildings where the soldiers, guards, and instructor soldiers slept. Along with the shelter, which would double as the eating area and class-room for the trainees, the two latrines, the command office building, and the four long mud-clay sleeping barracks, the only other structure in the area, standing out far from the others, was an old metal shipping container. The soldiers told the recruits that this container is where they would be locked up for misbehavior or attempts at escape.

The soldiers stopped the two lines of women when they arrived in front of one of the two buildings designated to be the recruit barracks. There were two tables set up in front of one of the barracks with an Eritrean officer sitting behind each table. The soldiers directed one recruit line in front of each table. The female conscripts reported to the officers one at a time. The officers had papers with the names of each of the recruits. The officers asked each recruit questions to fill out the forms, including birthdate, birthplace, parents' names, blood type (if known), allergies, education, height, weight, and any facial or body markings (as many Eritrean Eastern Orthodox women tattoo themselves including crosses on their foreheads and facial cheeks, hands, arms, and other locations). After the officer was finished asking each recruit the questions and filling in the forms, the recruit would move forward into the barracks. Inside the barracks, the soldiers gave each recruit a clean dry wool blanket; a compliment to the uniform they were already wearing including a khaki uniform short sleeve shirt, another pair of khaki shorts with large pockets on each leg, another cotton t-shirt; and a pair of foam rubber sandals.

The buildings were bare except for twenty foam mattresses on the floor of each building. Each of the two barracks had only one door and three windows in the front wall and three windows in the back wall, which provided ample light during the day. Each recruit was assigned a place with a foam mattress in the open-bay barracks to place their clothes, blanket, and their metal bowl. The soldiers put 14 recruits in one building and 13 in the other. This would be their home for the next two months. During this two-month period, the foam mattress, the wool blanket, the metal bowl, the uniform shirt, two pair of shorts, two t-shirts, and the pair of sandals would be each girl's only possessions.

The soldiers left the recruits alone in the barracks with instructions to place their blanket, bowl, and additional uniform neatly beside their mattress. They could rest on their mattress and talk to each other for a couple hours, but when they heard the whistle blow, they were to run outside the barracks as fast as possible and line up.

After the soldiers left the barracks, Sarah went to a window and looked out. From a window on the front wall, she could see most of the compound including the shelter where they had showered, slept, and ate breakfast. She also saw the Command Office and the soldiers' barracks. Sarah also noticed several guards standing in front of the barracks.

Sarah crossed the width of the barrack and looked out a window on the back wall. Looking straight out, all she could see was a few more guards standing watch on the backside of the barracks, and nothing else except miles and miles of dirt and rocks. As she leaned, tilting her head to see more, she could see in the distance the lone shipping container the guards had mentioned as the punishment holding area, looking frighteningly ominous in the distance.

Sarah went back to her mattress and lay down. She greeted the girls to her left and right. She rolled over to her knees beside her mattress and prayed. She thanked God she was now warm and dry, and out of the truck; she thanked God for the food she had eaten; and she asked for protection and strength for the difficult times she was sure lay ahead. Then, Sarah rolled back onto her mattress and fell asleep, a very deep sleep with dreams of her as a little girl chasing goats. A goat started to cry… the crying got louder and louder… the goat's crying was so loud… sounded like…

…a loud whistle blowing. Sarah woke up to a loud whistle blowing. A soldier was walking down the center of the barracks blowing a whistle. The girls were screaming and running for the door. Sarah jumped up and followed the recruits outside.

The soldiers were outside yelling as the females came running outside the barracks. They formed the new female recruits into two lines. A Sergeant stood to the side of the lines and told the recruits to stay in the lines, but turn toward him. Then he told them to raise their arms straight out to their sides and adjust the space between their comrade to their left and right. The Sergeant told them they were now "Trainees" and the trainees would come to this position every time the whistle is blown. He then blew the whistle again and told the trainees to go back into the barracks, get their metal bowl, and return to their positions as fast as possible. He blew the whistle again. The girls ran back into the barracks, retrieved their metal bowls, and returned to their spots.

When all the trainees were back in place, the Sergeant blew the whistle and a soldier standing on each side of the Sergeant demonstrated how to do jumping jacks exercises. The Sergeant told the women to begin doing the exercise. They did 50 jumping jacks. Then the soldiers demonstrated to the trainees how to do push-ups. The Sergeant blew the whistle and the soldiers got down into the push-up position; he blew the whistle again and they began doing push-ups as the Sergeant counted. He blew the whistle again and the soldiers jumped up to a standing position. The trainees stood up too. Then the Sergeant blew the whistle again as the soldiers screamed at the trainees to get down. The Sergeant counted as the women did 20 push-ups. He blew the whistle again and the trainees jumped up to a standing position. Then they went for a run through the rocky desert. They continued those activities for several hours until it was time to eat the evening meal of injera, beans, and water beneath the shelter.

The trainees were allowed about 30 to 40 minutes for eating and the escorted trips to the latrine. After they were finished eating, the soldiers sprayed water on the trainees. The soaking lasted about ten minutes and facilitated their combined shower, washing their clothes (some girls took their shirts off during the soakings to wring them out and wash them better), and washing their bowls. Then the trainees were released to go back to their barracks for the night. That was the beginning and context of the next two months of training.

Every morning, just as the sun was rising, the trainees' day began with a whistle blowing. The trainees ran outside to form their lines. They would march over to the shelter and receive a piece of injera and water in their bowl. The trainees would be allowed about 20 minutes to eat and be escorted to the latrine. Then they would form their lines and march back to the barracks. They would practice drill movements, do exercises of jumping jacks and push-ups, and run; do more drill movements, more exercises, and more running, for several hours. The sun would blaze on their heads from above and reflect back up from the desert rocks into their faces. They would only stop a few minutes after the drill movements for a water break. While they would be out running, the soldiers would fill their bowls with water for them. If their bowls were spilt during the exercising or movement drills, they would have to suffer their thirst until they returned from the next run. Some trainees would pass out and they would be left where they were by the group. Sometimes soldiers would come to carry them to the shelter and douse them with water until they recovered. If they recovered in a day, sometimes two, they were returned to training. Several trainees had passed out and recovered to be returned to training, but by the end of the first week, five girls were gone completely. They had passed out and did not return to training as most did. Sarah never knew if they had died or what happened to them. Rumors circulated that if the girls that failed training actually survived, but were too weak to complete training, the girls would be used by the soldiers in their barracks until they did die. In any case, these and other future girls dropped from training were never seen by Sarah again.

Sarah did well in this part of training. She adapted well to the heat and excelled in the exercises and running. Although she kept her position in the line while running, it was obvious to the soldiers that Sarah was one of the strongest trainees. While there were strict fraternization rules preventing the soldiers and guards from talking directly to the trainees except for corrections, some of the soldiers found moments to compliment Sarah on her performance.

Life during the first month was not bad for Sarah. She accepted her situation—she had food, water, a dry place to sleep, clothes, and she could talk to her new friends, the other trainees, a little in the evenings. Yes, she missed her life in the city, her family, and her old friends, but Sarah realized that God had saved her life several times and there must be a purpose for her in this world. She praised God for His Grace and asked for an opportunity to serve Him.

CHAPTER 6

EXERCISING FAITH

In the beginning, the first week or two, Sarah prayed quietly on her knees before going to sleep. Sometimes, if she woke before the soldiers came in blowing their whistles, she would pray before going out to start the day. As nights rolled on, Sarah became bolder in her praying and began praying out loud with ever increasing fervor. Sometimes, she would even sing praise songs and old Christian hymns she remembered from the underground Evangelical "Born Again" Church services and Bible study groups she used to attend. She tried to keep her voice down, but sometimes the Spirit would move her to be a little louder. Some of the other trainees would ask her about her faith and how she could worship and be happy. Sarah would pray with them and tell them they only needed to open the door for Christ to enter and give them the joy they were missing. Some of the girls were receptive and prayed with Sarah each night for one or two hours before going to bed. Some would even sing with her. Soon, about ten of the trainees prayed with Sarah and traded recitations of Bible verses they remembered. It was a blessed time for them and a good release from the days of stressful exercise and confinement. Sarah felt blessed in leading these girls to a more joyful and higher devotion to God.

As the group of trainees participating in the prayer group grew, their voices grew louder in the songs. They did not consider that there were guards standing outside the barracks and the guards were sure to have heard them. The guards seemed not to notice as Sarah and the trainees continued their prayer and praise time together each night. Each day rolled on into the next day, indistinguishable from another, exercising hot and hard during the days and Heaven-bound prayer and praise in the evenings. Nothing was said to Sarah or any of the trainees until near the end of the first month in the camp.

One night, a guard came in to the barracks as the ten or twelve trainees were on their knees praying; some were chanting their prayers, some were just shouting "Hallelujah," some were singing a praise song together. The guard came straight to Sarah in the middle of the group of trainees. He grabbed her arm, made her stand, and pushed her out of the barracks and on to the Command Building.

When the guard and Sarah arrived at the Command Building, he pushed Sarah inside and shut the door as he stayed outside by the door. The Commander sat behind the desk and looked up as Sarah fell to her knees after being pushed inside. She remembered the Commander from his speech when she first arrived in the camp even though she never remembered anything he had said on the first day. The Commander told Sarah that she was in violation of the rules by spreading "Born-Again Christianity", which was not authorized in Eritrea. Actually, no communications of any religion was authorized during the first two months of Eritrean military training. As the Commander was talking, Sarah became very frightened and tried to explain that she did not know these rules, but then she remembered a peace settling on her like God's Hand on her shoulder. She asked the Commander if he knew Jesus.? And if He had ever felt genuine peace? The Commander was stunned and didn't say anything for a minute. Sarah remembers that time felt like an hour or longer as he looked at her disbelieving the strength in her words. Sarah started to believe he was swayed by her conviction and thought about the stories of Daniel, Shadrach, Meshach, and Abednego she had read in her Bible. She thought the Commander was going to release her to go back to the barracks.

The Commander sentenced Sarah to stay a week in the shipping container. He called for the guard to come in and take Sarah to the container. He ordered the guard to give her injera once per day and one liter (about a quart) of drinking water twice per day. Sarah was crushed. She thought God would truly have saved her from this punishment considering she attempted to witness to the Commander. Sarah prayed as the guard pulled her from the small building. She felt the peace of God's Hand on her shoulder again. Sarah stood as tall as she could, although the guard was much taller than her, and she acted unafraid. She shook from the guard's hands and told him she could walk herself. Sarah stepped out in front of the guard and began walking toward the shipping container with the guard behind her. The lights from the eating and showering shelter lit up the area between it and the shipping container. Sarah could see it on the edge of the lighted area of the compound, shimmering in the moonlight, almost glowing. She walked proud across the field and entered the container. She felt brave.—She was brave, until the guard pushed her inside. The combination of artificial light and luminescence from the moon diminished as the guard closed the door and so did Sarah's courage. The overwhelming darkness surrounded her. She couldn't see at all. Sarah heard the guard bolt the latch on the outside of the door. She heard him walk away. She leaned against the container wall, still warm from the day's heat beating down on it, and slid to a seated position on the floor. It was dark. The container smelled like urine and death. She was alone. Sarah cried.

Sarah cried for a while; there was no way to tell how long she cried. But after a while, she asked herself why was she crying? Who would hear her crying? Who would see her tears? Sarah remembered her brothers telling her one time after beating her, that nobody cared to hear her poor sobs and crying would only give her a headache. But then she thought, God would hear her crying. But God already knew her situation; God had put His Hand on her shoulder and had given her strength before. Once again, she felt God was with her now, too. There must be a reason she had been placed into the shipping container. She was ok; she had not been beaten or hurt this time. Just as Daniel had been put into the lion's den; Shadrach, Meshach, and Abednego had been put into the fiery furnace; God did not keep them from being put inside; God protected them while they were inside! Praise God! Sarah felt God's strength and power and started to sing a praise song. She sang soft at first, gaining her strength, then louder. As she sang louder, she felt stronger and her spiritual darkness was overcome by visions of God's Glory.

Sarah got up on her knees and prayed, giving thanks for her health and God's amazing Power and Glory. "Even though I walk through the valley of the shadow of Death, I will fear no evil; for God is with me!" Sarah lay down and slept.

Sarah awakened feeling strange. It was dark. Perhaps it was still night. She was not sure where she was at first. Then, she saw small rays of sunlight coming through small holes in the walls near the top of the shipping container and lines of light coming through the edges of the door. Sarah was not sure what time it was, but she felt like she should be up exercising. She began to pray. As Sarah prayed, she could hear the other trainees outside running through the rocks of the desert floor. Although she wished she could be out running, showing off her speed to the other girls and the trainers, she was grateful for her health and extra time to praise God.

A guard came to the door and unbolted it. He yelled telling Sarah to stand back before he opened the large door at the end of the container. The light that rushed into the container as the guard opened the door hurt Sarah's eyes. The guard threw a piece of injera into the container and watched it land on the floor. He sat a liter bottle of water by the door. He told Sarah to come outside and escorted her to the small trainee latrine. Sarah used the bathroom and the guard escorted her back to the container. They walked past the shower shelter without stopping;—no shower for Sarah today. She picked up the liter bottle of water, entered the container, and picked up her injera. The guard shut and bolted the door. Sarah was in the dark again. Her eyes took some time to adjust to see her hands with the dim light filtering in from the small holes and the door. When she could see her injera, she raised it above her head, gave thanks to God for it, and ate.

As time passed through the day, as the sun rose high in the Eritrean desert sky, the sun beat down on top of the container; the rays of the sun reflected off the desert sand and rock surrounding the container generating intense heat onto the container's sides. The heat increased inside the shipping container. Sarah sweated, but prayed and sang hymns of praise. She remembered the time, just a little over a month ago, she was in another shipping container, along with other dead or dying girls. She remembered the smell of sweat, defecation, and death. She remembered the intense heat. She remembered her severe headache and vomiting so much. She prayed as she remembered, and praised God this was not as bad. She still smelled death and urine, but it was not so strong. She was stronger now, too, physically and spiritually. God was with her. She prayed for more strength and for her purpose to be revealed.

The day passed. Sarah snacked on the injera and the water a little at a time. The sun finally went down. A guard came, gave her another liter of water, took her to the latrine, escorted her back, and locked her back in the container. Sarah praised God she had survived the day. She prayed, sang songs of praise, prayed some more, and slept.

The next morning Sarah woke terrified. Nightmares of her youth, planes flying over shooting guns. The guns were so loud. Sarah screamed and awakened. But the guns were still firing. The horrifying noise was so loud inside the container. Sarah ran for the door and was trying to open it, but she couldn't. She was screaming so loud, but her screams only echoed inside the container. The gunshots were so terrifying to her. She screamed until a guard came and opened the container door. He laughed at her as she lay balled up in a heap, face between her knees, on the floor crying. The guard told Sarah it was only the trainees learning to shoot guns. If she were not in the container, she would be out on the firing range with the other trainees shooting too. The guard sat her liter of water down, threw her injera into the container, grabbed Sarah by her shoulders, and forced her to stand up. He escorted her to the latrine and back to the container. Sarah trembled as she walked and almost collapsed to hide on the ground each time another volley of gunfire sounded from the rifle range. After being bolted back into the shipping container, Sarah huddled into a corner and continued to cry. Eventually, she remembered to pray. Her prayers brought back the peace of God to her spirit. She began to sing praises and tried to be louder than the gunfire. The gunfire would stop for a few minutes then start back for a few minutes as another volley ensued. Sarah began to get the rhythm. She ate her injera, drank water, and prayed during the moments of quiet. She sang praises during the exploding firing of the guns. Finally, after several hours, the gunfire stopped for more than just a few moments; maybe the trainees were taking time for a training class, a long break or even lunch. Sarah was just glad for the extended quiet, time for a longer more meaningful prayer, and time to think. She thought of the timing of her punishment; how if she had not been placed in the container this week, she would have had to go to the rifle range with the other trainees; would she have been able to survive shooting a gun; she remembered her previous thoughts of why she couldn't be a soldier; she knew she could never shoot a gun; she could never shoot at a person; she would crumble every time she even heard a gun fire. Sarah praised God so much, so full of thanks for finding a way for her to miss the shooting exercises.

Then Sarah thought about when she would be released from the container at the end of the week; she would have to go to the ranges then. How would she be able to cope? Sarah hated the thought of being on the firing line, listening to the guns shooting on her left and right. She trembled at the thought of her actually holding and shooting a gun. And she cried when she thought she might actually have to point a gun at a person to kill them. She prayed for God to find a way out. God was with her and would help her. She had to escape. "Please God, be with me!"

Sarah continued to pray. It was quiet for a while and she used the quiet to meditate deeper and closer to God. She now realized that the trainees must have gone to the rifle range first, maybe after eating, before exercising, and were now out running. Later, probably after noon, the gunfire resumed and Sarah begin singing praise songs again, as loud as she could to help drown out the horrendous noise bombarding the container. She sang until her voice started to give out. Then the firing stopped. She could tell the sun was going down outside. She sang quietly now, to herself. Then she prayed until the guard came to get her empty liter bottle and give her another full bottle. She asked the guard if she could please go to the latrine. The guard hesitated, then agreed. He escorted Sarah to the latrine. Sarah looked in the direction of where the gunfire had been coming from. She was calmer now than she was this morning and could observe more. Although it was a getting dark, she could still see the mountains in the distance with red highlights as the sunset reflected off the rocky desert terrain. The rifle range must have been just two or three hundred meters out of the main compound in the direction of the mountains. She used the latrine and was escorted back to the container. It was very dark inside the container now. Sarah drank a little water, ate the rest of her injera from the morning, and prayed on her knees until she finally lay down and fell asleep still praying.

Sarah still remembers what she dreamt that night. She visualized her escape. She dreamed of how the shooting woke her up; how the guard came to give her the water and injera; everything she needed to do to escape. She saw everything clearly in her dream. Sarah woke up after the dream. It was late in the night, but she remembered the dream vividly and knew, with deep belief that God had given her this dream, exactly how her escape would happen. She thanked God for the plan and fell back asleep with a full confidence in God's mercy and power.

CHAPTER 7

ESCAPE

Sarah awoke to the sound of gunfire, just as she did in her dream. She still remembered every detail of the dream and she rehearsed the plan in her mind. She stood close to the door waiting for the guard to arrive. The guard always ordered Sarah to stand away from the door before he unbolted it. He would listen for her steps and reply before opening the door. Sarah was prepared. The guard came and told Sarah to stand back away from the door. Sarah made a few steps in place, then threw a small rock and some sand she had found in the corner of the container to the middle of the long container. Sarah then put her hands over her mouth and responded in a muffled, "Eweh" (Yes in Tigrinya). The guard lifted the latch on the door. Sarah placed her hands firmly against the door and prepared to push. The guard began pulling the heavy door open and Sarah pushed as hard as she could against the door. The door flew open fast and caught the guard off balance. The metal door hit him in the head and knocked him down. Sarah was already leaping out of the container carried by the inertia of her push. She almost tripped over the guard as he fell to the ground. Her agility allowed her to get a good footing in a crouched position on the other side of the guard's body, directly where he had laid down her liter bottle of water and injera. Sarah scooped up the water bottle and injera without wasting any extra time or motion and pounced up from her crouch like a cat running after a ball of twine. She knew the shooting range with the mountains behind was on her right side as she exited the container. The Trainee Barracks and Guard Barracks were respectively aligned and adjacent to her right. The Command Office was directly in front of her. And the Compound Gate with the road leading to Barentu was to her left. Sarah was prepared as she had seen her escape in her dream the night before. It was like acting out an action scene from a movie.

The guard just lay still on the ground. Sarah wasn't sure if he was just stunned, unconscious, or maybe even dead, but she didn't waste time to check. That had not been in her dream and she knew she could not worry about it at that moment. Sarah just jumped up and ran! She realized from her landing outside of the container, she was already facing to the left of the container door. Sarah didn't even have to turn as she leapt up and ran. She maneuvered a bit to her left keeping the long side of the container between her and the rifle range. She could hear the gunshots behind her. Sarah listened for any screaming behind her as she ran her usual running speed. She didn't hear any commotion at all, only the sporadic off and on gunfire volleys. Sarah knew she had to maintain her consistent speed for a long distance and she didn't want to push too hard so her breathing would not interfere with her hearing. She just did what she did best; Sarah ran, fast but steady.

Sarah turned slightly to the left after 200 meters, before she arrived at the gate because she feared there might be guards at the gate. There was also heavy fencing approximately 50 meters on either side of the gate she didn't want to have to jump. But the rest of the circumference of the compound was not fenced at all.

As she passed by the gate, approximately 100 meters to her right, she glanced over to it. Just as she remembered from her dream, the gate was not manned. Even those soldiers must have been needed on the rifle range for the trainees. Or maybe they were inside the guard shack sleeping, slumbering easy waiting for the sound of an upcoming vehicle from Barentu. All that mattered to Sarah was that she couldn't see anyone there, and hopefully, prayerfully, that meant that no one was there to see her or chase her. As she continued running past the gate and praising God for the absence of armed guards, or any guards there, she reprimanded herself for even fearing that there might be, because God showed her in her dream there wouldn't be. Praise God!

The road out of the gate ran north to Barentu. Sarah ran to the left adjacent to the gate, due west, for about 30 minutes. She calculated that should be about three miles from the gate.

Sarah turned hard left and ran south for over an hour at her normal fast and focused speed before slowing down and looking behind her. There was no one behind her. She didn't hear any yelling, no engine noises, and she didn't see any dust raised up in the distance behind her. She was sure she was not being chased yet. Sarah had heard the gunfire volleys for a while as she ran, but she couldn't hear them now. Perhaps she was too far to hear them, but she didn't think so. Most likely, they had stopped. It was very likely that they had discovered the knocked over guard and Sarah's escape by now. She just kept running, though a bit slower now. Sarah knew she would have to run for at least another hour before finding a cactus to hide behind and rest for a bit. She also kept in mind that the road from Barentu ran south to the training camp gate then circled around to the east, outside of the base on the opposite side she had been running on. The road continued south from the back side of the training base and should be at least 2 to 3 miles on her left side paralleling her escape route. Sarah was mostly running on automatic, just running south, singing praise songs in her head as she ran, but she was also thinking. She thought about her route. Sarah knew the road ran south from the military camp she was running from, all the way to the Ethiopian border. She would run south paralleling the road, but would have to be careful to stay off the road because the silty dust of the relatively smooth dirt road would show her footprints better than the rocky desert floor and be easier to track her. She also wanted to stay far enough off the road so she couldn't be seen by passing vehicles. Attempting to run relatively straight was not such a problem, but avoiding the road might be difficult as the road had large winding zig-zags between the hills across the rocky desert. She would have to stay alert. Sarah praised God and continued to run.

Sarah somehow remembered, perhaps from seeing a map of Eritrea in the Commander's office or somewhere else in her memory, or perhaps an imposed image in her mind as a gift from God, that there was a river south of Barentu, about halfway to the Ethiopian border. Sarah knew she would have to cross the river and run for about 15 miles on the other side to the border. She would have to find a desolate place to cross the border.

Sarah ran for over an hour at full speed after leaving the training camp, then she made the conscious decision to slow down a bit to save her strength. She continued running for over another two hours at a slower, more efficient rate, and thought she should be coming to the river soon. Her body was getting weak from not eating and not drinking. Even being acclimated to the sparse diet and heavy exercise as her normal routine for the past month, she was beginning to feel over exerted with a great need to eat and rest a bit.

She saw a huge cactus and slowed to a walk to cool down her legs before arriving to it. Sarah sat down in the shade of the cactus and sipped a little of the water from her bottle. She ate half the injera and closed her eyes for a few minutes. She daydreamed she was at the foot of Christ's Cross looking up at her Savior. She could feel the aura of His glory surrounding her. Sarah looked up at Christ; His eyes were full of love and mercy. Christ told Sarah she would be well. Sarah felt a drop of His sweat, mixed with His Holy Blood land on her cheek. She opened her eyes and saw the shaded side of the cactus. A few drops of morning dew still hung from a sun shaded arm of the cactus. Another drop landed on Sarah's face and she felt as if God was blessing her. Sarah scratched at the cactus, clawed out a big chunk, and ate it. She knew the cactus would give her additional hydration and minerals her body was lacking. She took a couple big drinks of water from her bottle and finished the injera. Sarah waited another five to ten minutes listening to see if she could hear anything… . Nothing. She felt stronger now. She stood up and looked behind her direction of movement to see if there was any movement or dust rising… Nothing. Praise God!

Sarah turned and looked south to continue running. She ran at a moderate pace, trying to stay on track as the sun was getting high in the sky and it was becoming hard to judge direction. Sarah studied the horizon as she ran beneath the hot Eritrean sun, over the rocky desert. Her sweat ran down her forehead, stinging as it entered her eyes. Her vision was blurring from the sun and her sweat, but all there was to see were rocks and sand anyway.

CHAPTER 8

THE CABBAGE TREE

Sarah crested a small hill and looked down. She thought she could see a tree far off in the distance. Sarah wiped her eyes. Yes, it was a tree. Maybe it was a cabbage tree. Something was telling her in her mind it was a cabbage tree. She didn't know how she knew it was a cabbage tree; she had never seen a cabbage tree before or didn't even know how she even knew a thing like a cabbage tree existed. She just knew it was, and she knew the leaves and flowers of the cabbage tree would make her strong, and she knew it grew on the banks of the river. Perhaps, like the location of the river she didn't know she knew about, the identification of this cabbage tree was also a gift from God. Praise God Indeed!

Sarah ran to the cabbage tree. It was, indeed, growing on the bank of a river. She reached up and grabbed some leaves and flowers and ate them. The leaves were sweet and the flowers tasted like something she remembered eating at her grandmother's when she was young, mixed with Shiro Wat, a vegetarian dish eaten with injera. It was nice beneath the shade of the cabbage tree with a cool breeze coming up off the river. Sarah rinsed off in the cool water at the edge of the river while hiding beneath a tall embankment. She rested for a while and thought how very nice it would be to have a house right here beside the cabbage tree and the river. She knew she could not stay there very long, but it was early afternoon now and the hottest part of the day. Sarah stayed between the cabbage tree and the river for approximately three hours. She kept hidden from the direction the guards would be coming from by the high embankment. She dozed a bit from time to time, but very lightly, keeping her hearing sharp for the sounds of anything approaching. Sarah felt safe in the Arms of God and remembered God's promise of a table set before her in the presence of her enemies (Psalm 23: 5).

As Sarah sat reclined beneath the shade of the cabbage tree next to the river praising God, she thought of her future. During the past weeks, she had not thought about her future, not in a good positive light. Her future had looked dark. But now, the sky was clearing. God was her future and it was bright with His glory. Sarah thought about one day, she could be sitting like this, beneath the shade of a tree, beside a river, watching her son play in the water or run across the field on the river's bank. She also thought about her past and what brought her here. Sarah knew she had to keep God first in her life and God would reward her. God would always protect her and she could count her years as she tells the story of how God saved her. Counting her years.... Yes... oh, Sarah thought about her years... Yes! Her birthday! Something she had not thought of for months. Her birthday was near. She didn't know what exact day it was now, but she knew it had to be close to her birthday. Sarah was 19 years old now. Perhaps her 19th birthday was one of the days in the container. Or perhaps, it is even this very day, the day of her escape, the day of her enjoying this peace with God beneath the cabbage tree she hadn't known before, beside the river she hadn't known before. Yes, this must be her birthday.

"Happy Birthday, Sarah."
Blessings from God.
"Thank you so very much, God!"
Love and Praise,
Sarah

Time was moving and she knew she had to leave. She felt strong now from the injera and the cabbage tree leaves and flowers. She was also hydrated and rested now. Sarah filled her pockets with cabbage tree leaves and flowers, filled her liter bottle with fresh water from the river, and began looking for a good place to cross the river.

Sarah did not know how to swim. She hoped she could find a spot shallow enough where she could walk across, but she did not want to take a long time looking for a shallow spot. She might have to chance trying to swim across. She went to the narrowest spot she could see and waded out into the water. It went to her neck about half way across, so she came back to where it was at her waist and she walked downstream a bit. She tried walking out again, but again it went to her neck within a few steps. She went back a few steps and again moved downstream a bit more to try again. Each time the water touched her chin and she could feel the current below start to shift her feet out from under her, she could feel the fear of the river build up within her. Sarah began to cry and asked God to help her. She remembered the Israelites at the Red Sea when they were being chased by the Egyptians and thought how they felt. Then she knew God would help her like he had helped them. Just then, a tree branch came floating down stream and Sarah grabbed it. She pushed off the river floor and held on to the branch. She couldn't feel the bottom beneath her feet, but the branch supported her as she knew God was carrying her. The current carried her to the far side of the river until she could feel the ground beneath her feet again. Sarah used the branch to steady her as she climbed up the riverbank. She looked back across the river. She had floated so far downstream she couldn't even see the cabbage tree. She knew that would help her too; if they were able to track her to the cabbage tree, they wouldn't know where she got out of the river. Sarah ran about 100 meters south of the river and fell to her knees. She prayed giving God praise for being with her, guiding her, and carrying her.

Sarah stayed kneeling for a few minutes, trying to control her breathing, listening if anyone had followed her across the river. When her breathing was normal and there were no sounds, Sarah took the cabbage tree leaves and flowers out of her pockets, ate some and put the rest on the ground. She took her shorts off and rung the water out so the shorts would not be so heavy and they would not rub her raw so fast. She knew they would finish drying in the heat of the desert afternoon soon anyway. She put the shorts back on, reloaded the cabbage tree leaves into her pockets, and started running again. Sarah felt fresh and she resumed her normal speed. She had approximately 15 miles to go until she reached the Ethiopian border. Sarah knew if she could continue her pace, it would take her three to five hours to reach the border. She thought it must have been about 2 or 3 in the afternoon now; that would put her at the border around sunset. That would be perfect to cross if she took time to make sure no one was around, if she even knew exactly where the border was when she crossed. The border was not marked in most places and only fenced about 100 meters on either side of road gates. She knew she could find a place with no fences and no guards, but she would have to be careful to avoid landmines. Sarah had heard stories of small landmines for people and large landmines for cars and trucks all along the border between Eritrea and Ethiopia. She prayed as she ran. She also sang praise songs in her mind so as to not disturb her breathing. Sarah felt good. She felt fresh, confident, and strong. Sarah knew God was with her.

Sarah ran for what she calculated to be a little over two hours. Although she had previously thought she would have been able to keep running until she arrived at the border, her legs were getting tired and her overall energy and strength were getting weak. Sarah slowed, but kept running. She ran for another 30 minutes at the slower pace and decided to stop for a short rest in the wide shadow of a tall cactus. Looking at the position of the sun, she thought it must be about 4 or 5 P.M. The sun would be down in a couple hours. Sarah ate the rest of the cabbage tree leaves and flowers and drank the rest of her water. She sat behind the cactus for about 30 minutes. The last 10 or 15 minutes behind the cactus she spent on her knees praying, thanking God for bringing her safely this far and asking God's favor to continue to give her strength, direction, and protection. Sarah took off running again, but at the slower pace now. She could tell the sun was falling in the western sky to her right, so she knew she was still running south. And she also knew that God was still with her.

After running just about 20 minutes, Sarah saw the silhouettes of two people and a cow walking perpendicular to her direction of running. She slowed down but kept running closer. As she neared the people, she could tell that they were two young boys, one perhaps 12 or 14 years old and the other a few years younger. She ran up to them, slowing to a walk just a few steps from meeting them, and greeted the boys. Sarah told them her name was "Semhar" and asked them their names. She asked them where they were coming from and where they were going. The boys greeted Sarah back and seemed anxious to talk to a stranger on this long road. The older boy, Yeshua, was about the same height as Sarah and seemed especially eager to talk to this beautiful young woman. They stopped walking and Yeshua told "Semhar" that he and his brother had come from their village outside the small town of Shambiko. They were taking their cow to sell at the market in Badme. They were going to spend the night in Badme with an uncle, sell the cow the next day in the market, and return to Shambiko. Sarah knew that Badme is a large trading town on the border between Eritrea and Ethiopia. Sarah told the boys that she was from Badme and she was in training to run the marathon in the Olympics for Eritrea. The boys were very excited to hear this and they began talking.

Yeshua seemed interested in "Semhar's" military style shorts with big pockets and asked her if they were easy to run in. "Semhar" told Yeshua that they were the only shorts her father would allow her to run in until she was approved for the Olympic Team because the shorts were long and at least covered her upper legs. However, she continued, they didn't protect her well from the sand flies; as it was late in the afternoon already, she wished she had a pair of loose trousers like Yeshua was wearing. Yeshua asked if "Semhar" wanted to trade? Sarah could see the lust in Yeshua's eyes because he really wanted those military style shorts. "Semhar" hesitated a bit, because she needed the shorts to continue to train. But… after thinking, "Semhar" told Yeshua she did have another pair at home and it would be selfish not to grant him his wish. Just down the road a bit, Sarah saw two thick juniper bushes, so she told Yeshua, if he really wanted to trade, they could go down to those bushes and swap. However, "Semhar" continued to act like she wasn't sure about the trade and asked if the boys had anything to eat. They had some dried beef sticks and Yeshua said that he would include those in the trade. They agreed and went down the road to the Juniper bushes. Yeshua went behind one bush and "Semhar" went behind the other bush. Yeshua threw her his trousers and "Semhar" threw him her shorts. The shorts were just a little loose on Yeshua, but he knew he would grow into them soon. He was very happy. The pants fit Sarah's waist, and, as they were made to be loose and airy, they fit her everywhere else too. Yeshua gave "Semhar" half of the bag of dried beef sticks he had. "Semhar" told the boys she had to finish her run before it got dark so she had to go. The boys continued walking southwest to Badme and Sarah jumped over the berm of the road and ran south. She ran as fast as she could now to get distance from the road and the boys. Sarah was so thankful to God for the opportunity to trade her military shorts for a pair of common trousers. She had not thought of it before, but it would have been difficult to explain her military shorts in any town of either Eritrea or Ethiopia. Sarah thought it would be easy to explain her tank top and she could easily find a shawl to cover her head and chest in any market. She held her empty water bottle in one hand and her beef sticks in the other hand. Sarah ran and started singing praise songs out loud. She didn't care if the singing disturbed her breathing now; Sarah wanted God and all His creation to hear her praise for His mercy and glory.

Sarah continued to run south for another hour. The sun was almost down to the horizon on her right side and she could see red reflections off distant mountains on her left side. The sky was a deep dark greyish blue. She knew she would have to stop running now and find a place to sleep. She shouldn't run at night because it would be too easy to lose direction without the sun. It would also be dangerous because she could step in a hole or trip on a rock and hurt herself. Sarah could not even imagine what would happen to her now if they found her there with a broken leg or even a sprained ankle, which would keep her from running further. And with the border getting close, Sarah needed to be alert with good visibility to watch for guards and landmines.

CHAPTER 9

NOOG FLOWERS

Sarah found a thick patch of *noog* flowers (also known as ramtil or blackseed—a tall stem leafy bright yellow aster flower). She picked several of the leafy plants on the southern end of the patch and carried them to the middle of the patch. She picked several of the plants from the middle of the patch and lay down where they had been. Sarah got back up on her knees and prayed thanking God for always watching over her, keeping her safe so far, and she praised God for His mighty grace and mercy. She ate half of her beef sticks then lay back down and covered herself with the plants she had picked. The air was already starting to chill and there was a cool wind blowing across the desert terrain. But the patch of noog flowers was enough to block the wind and the picked leaves and flowers, smelling so sweet, was enough to keep her warm. She was so tired. She would fall asleep quick. Sarah started drifting off to sleep as she thought about the day. It had been such a long day, with Sarah running so far, with her finding only blessings along the way. Just before she fell asleep, she looked up at the moon shining down on her with its beautiful glowing surface and the shadows of its imperfections making it so lovely. She was amazed at the vast multitude of stars glistening. She remembered a Psalm (136): "Give Thanks to the Lord, for He is good! His Love Endures forever!... Who made the great lights – His Love endures forever!... the moon and stars to govern the night! His Love endures forever!" Sarah slept.

Sarah woke as the sun was coming up. She was a bit cold, but not too much. She sat up and looked around in the morning light. The patch of noog flowers she slept in enhanced the dawn with their beautiful yellow color and they smelled so wonderful. Sarah thought it was strange, though, as she looked around, that there were no other patches of flowers. Actually, there was nothing around for miles. She could see mountains in the distance, near the horizon, and rolling hills. There may have been some acacia trees or juniper bushes in the distance, too, but she wasn't sure because of the morning haze. She thought it was a tremendous blessing that this isolated patch of noog flowers was exactly in her path and she came across it exactly when she needed a place to sleep. Sarah repositioned herself to her knees and prayed, thanking God for keeping her safe through the night and sharing this glorious morning with her. She asked God to continue to watch over her and to protect the trainee girls she left behind.

Some of the noog flowers had gone to seed. Sarah knew that the seeds would be good to protect her from getting sick. She grabbed a handful of seeds, found a rock, and smashed the seeds to powder. She licked the powder from her hand. It was bitter and she knew not to take too much, but she felt like it made her a bit stronger. She ate the rest of her beef sticks to quench her hunger a bit and to get rid of the taste of the crushed seeds. She looked around a bit longer for any signs of people and listened to hear anything. She could see for miles in all directions. She didn't see anything dangerous for her and all she could hear was the wind.

Sarah saw the sun rising over the mountains in the eastern distance to her left. She started running south. She ran at a good pace, not as fast as she did starting out yesterday, or even as fast as she did after she rested beneath the cabbage tree, but still a good rate of speed. Sarah thought she should be at the border within an hour or two. She kept a careful watch, continuously cycling her eyes from left to right, down at the ground in front of her, and toward the horizon as she ran, searching for signs of the border, for people, for dust clouds, and especially for landmines.

After running approximately two hours, maybe longer, Sarah came to a dirt road crossing the direction of her running. She stopped short of the dirt road and went to a large acacia tree. Sarah lay down on her stomach to hide behind the tree. She wanted to observe the road for a while before crossing it. Soon, she saw some people with a mule pulling a wagon coming down the road. Sarah waited for them to pass without letting them see her. A woman was leading the mule with a little boy and a little girl sitting on the wagon. The wagon had several large plastic containers of water on it. After the wagon passed and moved further down the road a couple hundred meters, Sarah ran after them. Sarah began yelling at them when she got to within 20 meters of them... "Hello! Hello! Good Morning!"

Sarah approached the woman with polite respectful greetings. The woman stopped the mule when she heard the young woman calling out to her. Sarah introduced herself to the woman as "Salam" and told the woman she was lost. She told the woman that her father had woken her up early in the morning to tell her one of their few sheep had gotten out of the pen overnight. He had work to do and needed "Salam" to go out and find the sheep. She had left her father's house without eating breakfast and grabbed a water bottle that was almost empty. "Salam" started to cry and told the woman she had gotten lost, was hungry and thirsty. The woman felt sorry for "Salam" and told her she could fill her water bottle from their water. The woman also gave "Salam" a piece of injera, which was accepted graciously. "Salam" thanked the woman over and over. The woman told Sarah that they had just come from the town of Hiret after getting water for the week and were going home now. They lived just off this road close to the border crossing. The woman told "Salam" very proudly that her husband was a guard at the border crossing. The lady continued to talk, seemingly glad to have someone to talk to. Sarah listened to the woman talk for a while and gathered all the information the woman provided. Sarah had never heard of the town of Hiret. She did not know of any town this close to the border except Badme, where the boys she passed yesterday were going. Sarah listened to the woman in confusion for a while, until she realized she was actually already in Ethiopia. She must have crossed the border into Ethiopia without knowing it.

Sarah was so happy, overjoyed! She wanted to shout praises to God right there! She was in Ethiopia and she was only a few miles from a town where nobody knew her or would be looking for her. Halleluiah! Sarah screamed to herself as the woman continued to talk about her home and the market in the town of Hiret. Sarah was only half listening now as she thought about how good God had been to her and what she would do when she arrived in Hiret. Only by the grace of God, she was able to keep her excitement inside for a moment. She knew she had to stay a bit calm or the woman would know something was not right. With the woman's husband being a border crossing guard, she might turn Sarah in. When the woman stopped talking for a second, Sarah could not contain herself any longer. "Salam" shouted, "Praise God! Yes, I know Hiret! My father's house is near there and I can get to his house from there! Thank you so much!"

"Salam" thanked the woman again, told her good-bye and that she hoped they met again. Sarah started walking down the road toward Hiret, in the opposite direction of the woman, children, and donkey cart. Sarah ate the injera and drank some water as she walked. After the injera was finished and the woman was far enough down the road, Sarah started running toward the town. Sarah praised God as loud as she could! Sarah sang praise songs to God as she ran, not worried about her breathing, not worried about noise, running on the road not worried about dust or footprints, just happy to be a child of God.

Sarah passed a few family compounds along the road. People working gardens or moving sheep and goats hardly paid any attention to Sarah at all as she ran by. She saw the edge of the town of Hiret after about fifteen minutes from leaving the woman and her children. Sarah slowed to an easy walk to calm her breathing and gain a better posture for people to see as she entered the town. She would be in town within five more minutes at this pace. She continued her earlier thoughts of what she would do when she arrived in town. Sarah bowed her head a bit, closed her eyes as she walked down a straight portion of the road, and prayed for forgiveness for the necessary lies she told and for God to give her a good story and the right words to say.

CHAPTER 10

HIRET

Sarah walked into the town of Hiret. She tried not to look left or right too much; tried to act like she knew where she was going; like she belonged there. She knew she was still not safe. She could still be caught and returned to Eritrea. Especially this close to the border, there were probably many people with family in Eritrea, Eritrean traders, and even, especially, Eritrean military spies. She realized the dangers; however, Sarah still walked with the confidence that God was protecting her.

Sarah felt conscientious and vulnerable in the bright openness of the road. She felt everyone was watching her. She put her head down a bit and even hunched her shoulders forward. She wanted to look a bit younger than she was and she didn't want her braless breasts to draw attention through the thin, form fitting, sweaty tank top she was wearing. Sarah knew with the khaki color of the tank top and her olive skin tone, it might look like she was topless. She would have to get a shawl or blouse as soon as she could. She went beneath the canopies of the first market area she came upon. It was shaded beneath the thick cloth canopies flapping in the breeze. It was still before midday, so the market was not so crowded yet. Sarah felt a little more comfortable in the darker and closer confines between the tables in the market. Many of the tables were bare as some venders were still setting up in preparation for the afternoon crowds. Sarah moved around between the tables beneath the shaded canopies. She stopped at one table that was being stocked. The merchant woman had left some dress wrap cloths lying on the table while she went to her shed to get more. Sarah held one up and looked at it. It would be easy to take off running with it. She was sure she could get away before the lady returned and no one else would notice her. She could hide somewhere to give her time to wrap it around her so she could look more presentable. She was thinking of it and even visualizing it in her mind. She could do it. But, no! Sarah could not steal this cloth. She was not a child; and God had helped her and protected her so far; Sarah remembered her values and God confirmed in her heart and mind, "Thou shalt not steal!" Sarah could not disobey; she could not violate this Commandment. But it was so tempting. She knew she needed to change her appearance. Sarah was still standing there, holding the cloth up, thinking of running, praying for strength to avoid the temptation, when the woman returned. Sarah was grateful to God not to extend the temptation further. She had thought and prayed many times in the container that God would not make us go through more than we could handle without Him. God would be there and come to us in our struggles. God was there with Sarah.

The woman asked Sarah if she wanted to buy the cloth. Sarah told her that it was beautiful and she really needed it, but she did not have any money. Sarah told the woman that her clothes and money had been stolen, which was not a real lie as they had been taken from her. The woman asked Sarah if she would be willing to work for the cloth. Sarah smiled at the woman and thanked her for the offer. She agreed to work the rest of the day for the cloth. Sarah told the woman her name was "Salam," same as she told the woman on the road, in case that woman saw and recognized her when she came back to town. The vendor woman told "Salam" she had other tables in the market she had to watch. She normally had another girl watch one or two tables for her, but that girl had not showed up for work today. Sarah wrapped the cloth around her and helped the woman finish stocking the tables. Sarah thanked God for the cloth, for the work, for the kindness of the woman, and for the opportunity to establish relationships in this town. God is surely Good!

Sarah ran between two tables selling cloths from each for the rest of the day. At the end of the day, the woman told "Salam" she did a good job and gave her a little money from the day's profits. She told "Salam" she could return the next morning and perhaps the woman could use her again. Sarah walked away from the tented market area, down a small road to a large opening in the center of town. It was late in the day. The sun was going down but the air was still very hot. Sarah saw a cloth pitched and tied to hay bales where some young women were eating.

Market area in Karen, Eritrea (Photo by Tredway)

Sarah went over to the girls, introduced herself as "Salam," and asked if they had room for her. The girls welcomed "Salam" into their group and shared their injera and vegetables with her. These girls were from nearby villages and came to the town to work during the week. They did not have a place to stay in the town so they found hay bales to sleep between at night. Sarah felt comfortable and safe with them. She listened to their stories of their day as they ate and laughed together. Before she ate, Sarah bowed her head and prayed to herself. After eating, the girls continued to talk while their new friend "Salam" continued to listen. It was difficult for Sarah not to talk, but she thought it was best if she just pretended to be shy and quiet. The sun went down and the girls started to fall asleep. Sarah moved to the edge of a bale, a few meters away from the girls, went to her knees, and prayed a long prayer of thanksgiving to God for all His love and protection. Sarah went back to the girls huddled up to stay warm in the night air and lay down to sleep, still with prayers of praise singing in her heart and mind. Glory to God! Amen!

"Salam" stayed in the Ethiopian town of Hiret for eight days. She went to work for the vendor woman every morning. The vendor woman let "Salam" work for her every day, except for two of those days because the other girl was working for her too and those two days there was not enough work for both girls. The vendor woman paid "Salam" good wages for the little work and gave her breakfast and lunch. Even on the two days the vendor woman told "Salam" she didn't have work for her, the vendor woman still gave "Salam" injera and beans for breakfast and a little money for lunch.

Sarah bought another cloth wrap, a blouse, a skirt, and a pair of sandals to have a change of clothes and look more like the other girls. Since the vendor woman was giving her breakfast and lunch, she didn't need to buy food. Sarah gave the other girls she was sleeping with a little money for the food they shared with her. Sarah saved the rest of the money for transportation she knew she was going to need when she left the small town of Hiret that had welcomed her and been so good to her. Although "Salam" felt comfortable in Hiret with her new friends, Sarah knew she had to leave before someone reported her to the authorities. She could not risk them sending her back to Eritrea.

On the morning of her eighth day in Hiret, "Salam" told the vendor woman and her friends that she had to go visit her sick aunt in Gondor (a large Ethiopian city south of Hiret). She gave them all very sincere thanks, especially the vendor woman, and told them she would be back in a month or two. Sarah went to the area of town known as the tax-park (taxi/bus staging area) to wait for a bus. But Sarah did not get on the bus for Gondor. She hid and waited a couple of hours for the bus to Axum (aka Aksum, another large Ethiopian city east of Hiret). She boarded the bus, and on that eighth afternoon, Sarah said goodbye to Hiret. She cried as the bus left the town. God and Hiret had been very good to her and she praised God for all His wonders in her life. Sarah kept her head up for a while going down the dirt road. She saw where she had first gotten on the road and met the woman and the children with the donkey cart before walking into Hiret. Sarah looked out to the north, in the direction she had run from Eritrea. She wondered if they had even pursued her that far, maybe to the border? Maybe only to the river? It didn't matter now. It was all past. God had kept her safe and God would continue to protect her. Sarah bowed her head low praying. She also stayed low because she knew she would be passing adjacent to the border crossing road soon. She kept her head low and sang praises to God all the way to Axum.

CHAPTER 11
THE QUEEN OF SHEBA

Although it was only approximately 100 miles straight-line distance from Hiret to Axum, it would take several hours to get there. The bus would have to travel on a dirt road southeast winding through mountain passes for three to four hours, then go northeast up a paved road for another two to three hours. Although Axum was close to the Eritrean border, Sarah thought she would be safe there for a while. Axum would be a big enough city she would not draw attention. Sarah could get a job there and have time to think about where she would go next. Sarah had heard a lot about Axum in school. Axum was the heart and history of her people.

Axum was the original birthplace of the ancient Abyssinian (Ethiopian) Empire (which includes Eritrea). The Queen of Sheba, mentioned in the Holy Bible as the most beautiful woman in the world, was from Axum. The Queen of Sheba conquered the heart of the Israeli King Solomon. Sheba and Solomon were in such deep love, the Song of Solomon (aka Song of Songs) in the Old Testament of the Bible, was written of them. The Queen of Sheba bore a son to King Solomon, Prince Menelik. Sheba, and the people of Abyssinia, had worshiped the Sun prior to her marriage to King Solomon. Sheba was so captivated with Israel, the people, and their love and worship of their God, when she took Prince Menelik back to Abyssinia, she took Judaism, the religion of Israel, back with her. The people of Abyssinia began to worship the God of Israel and studied the Laws of Moses. When the Queen of Sheba died, Prince Menelik ruled Abyssinia as the first Ethiopian Emperor and was known as "Great Unifier of the Abyssinian Kingdoms" and the "Lion of Judah." The Lion of Judah rock carving Emperor Menelik created at the top of one of the highest mountains surrounding Axum after he was anointed Emperor still exists.

Emperor Menelik's 3000-year-old carving of The Lion of Judah outside Axum, Ethiopia (Photo by Tredway)

The 3000-year old foundation to the Queen of Sheba's Palace also still stands on the outskirts of Axum.

The foundation ruins of the Queen of Sheba's Palace outside Axum, Ethiopia (Photo by Tredway)

The roaring of the bus engine, the wheels rolling on the desert road, the heat, and the stale air of the bus soon put Sarah to sleep. She was praying as she fell asleep and dreamed she was at the foot of the Cross of Jesus with Mary (Jesus' mother), Mary Magdalene, and Salome (the wife of Zebedee and mother of James and John). Sarah was crying with the other women as tears from their eyes mixed with drops of blood from Christ's beaten body. Tears flowed down Sarah's face. Soldiers came and pushed the women away from the cross. Sarah was jostled from side to side; she could feel the sweaty arms of the soldiers as they pushed against her. She awakened to find herself in her seat, being pushed and jostled by the sweaty people sitting near her in the small bus. The paved road they were on for a while had ended and this unpaved road was extremely bumpy here as the bus neared the city of Axum. Sarah praised God she had gone unnoticed past the border crossing and was close to a city big enough to get lost and stay unnoticed in.

Sarah looked out the window as the bus entered Axum. She was amazed at some of the newer buildings and construction. She didn't expect Axum to be this big. The paved roads, the old and new buildings side by side, the slums, the market, and construction sites reminded her of Asmara, the capital of Eritrea, and when she would walk the streets there. Sarah got off the bus when it stopped at the city center tax-park. She had paid her bus fare before entering the bus at Hiret, but gave the bus driver a small tip as she got off here. Sarah still had enough money to buy food for a few days. She walked around the corner from where the bus stopped, knelt on her knees and prayed thanks to God for bringing her safe so far and asked God that she could get a job soon. Praise God! Amen!

Sarah walked around town for about an hour as evening descended. The sky began to get dark, but the city center was lit up by hotel and restaurant lights. Sarah went into a few hotels to ask for a job. She found her way to the back of each hotel and asked cleaning girls that were changing their clothes as they finished their work for the day. Most of the girls told her to return in the morning. At one hotel, one cleaning girl told Sarah that the manager was still at the front desk and she should talk to him. Sarah went around to the front of the hotel and talked to the manager. The manager told Sarah he didn't actually need a new cleaning girl for the hotel, but the hotel owner was looking for a good cleaning girl for his home. He told Sarah that he would tell the owner about Sarah and she should come around noon the next day to meet the owner. The manager asked Sarah if she had eaten. Sarah told him she had just come on the bus from Gondor and had not eaten since she had a piece of injera for breakfast. He told her it was still early for the staff to eat dinner, but if she could return to the hotel in an hour, at 8 P.M., she could eat with the staff. Sarah thanked him gratefully and walked around the city some more. She returned to the hotel and ate a good dinner with the staff, injera with fried "tibs" (beef cubes), lintels, and vegetables. It was more than she had eaten in a long time. She ate well, but not too much, as she did not want to be rude or appear to be so desperate. She listened to the staff talk and laughed with them. It was nice, like sitting with the girls amid the haystacks in Hiret. She introduced herself as Sarah (she felt safe using her real name here) but told them of the hard life she had been living since her parents died and she had to live with her uncle in Gondor; how he forced her to overwork and how he beat her when he was drunk. One of the cleaning girls, named Genet, told Sarah she could stay with her for the night. Genet and Sarah left the hotel staff room together and walked through the city a bit. Genet showed Sarah some of the good hotels and res- taurants, as well as places to stay away from while looking for a job.

They went to where Genet stayed, a small corrugated metal lean-to shack.

Girls' Market Kiosk and home in Asbe Tefera, Ethiopia
(Photo by Tredway)

Inside was just enough room for a small bed, a small table, and a shelf that had a few pieces of clothes, a couple handbags, a few pairs of shoes, and a bucket. Genet showed Sarah where the borehole (water pump) was outside. Next to the borehole was a concrete pad, surrounded by a tall cloth drape, where they could take a bucket shower. They took their respective turn using the bucket to shower. Genet let Sarah shower first and assured her she would stand watch outside the cloth curtain for her. The shower felt good. Sarah dried, wrapped her cloth around her, and stood watch outside the curtained concrete pad for Genet as she showered. The girls walked back to Genet's shelter and lay down in the bed together. Genet got on the bed first and lay pushed against the back wall. It was very generous for Genet to share her limited space with Sarah. Sarah was extremely grateful. She told Genet how very much she appreciated her and then rolled out of the bed onto her knees and prayed. She thanked God for His protection and for providing Sarah with so much love, for her new friend, Genet, and for the prospect of a job. Life was good and God is great! When she finished praying, she got back in bed. Genet was already asleep. Sarah lay on her side beside Genet, ensuring not to push on Genet, while also careful not to fall off the bed. She used the small plastic bag filled with her few items clothes as a pillow. Sarah praised God until she fell asleep, too.

Sarah slept well. She and Genet woke up together. Sarah prayed as Genet took a quick shower. They walked back to the hotel together and ate some injera with the other cleaning girls. The cleaning girls organized and began their working day. Sarah walked around Axum. She saw a clock tower and checked with it about every hour until 11 A.M. Sarah went back to the hotel lobby and saw the manager. The manager told her he had told the owner of her looking for a job. The owner had said he would be there about 1 P.M. to meet with Sarah. The manager ordered a juice for Sarah and she sat in the lobby reading magazines, mostly Ethiopian tourism guides, and drinking the delicious juice, something she had not had in such a very long time, waiting on the owner.

Sarah also prayed as she waited. The hotel owner came a little after 1 P.M. After talking to the hotel manager, the owner took Sarah to his office. He introduced himself as Isaias. He asked Sarah about her life and experience. Sarah told Isaias she had graduated secondary school in Gondor and told him the same story she had told the cleaning staff the previous day, about her parents dying and her having to live with her abusive uncle, her running away and coming to Axum. She assured the owner she was 19 years old, but she had left her identity card at her uncle's in Gondor. Although Sarah hated lying, she knew she could not tell the truth about escaping from Eritrea. She would be illegal in Ethiopia until she could officially file for asylum or refugee status. Sarah would have to be careful until she found out how to do that.

CHAPTER 12

ISAIAS AND ESTHER

Isaias was nice and seemed to be sympathetic to Sarah. He was an older man, older than her own father. He told Sarah that he and his wife lived alone. They had a son that lived in Gondor. The hotel owner's wife, Esther, couldn't walk; she used a wheelchair to get around a bit, but she could not clean the house. Their previous housekeeper moved away. Isaias talked to Sarah for about an hour. Sarah let him do most of the talking so she would not have to keep lying. The hotel "Coffee Girl" came into the owner's office and gave them each a cup of coffee and some popcorn. All Ethiopian hotels and most restaurants have a "Coffee Girl." Coffee is considered magical in Ethiopia, a gift of God, and there are very specific methods of preparing and serving it. Ethiopian coffee (more like Expresso)is served from a pot on a burner with incensed coals. And it is always served with popcorn. The texture and saltiness of the popcorn complements the flavor of the extra thick Ethiopian coffee. Isaias inhaled deeply taking in the strong aroma before he sipped his coffee. Sarah also savored the deep rich flavor. Sarah felt the hotel owner studying her as they drank their coffee. Sarah drank her coffee a bit slower than Isaias. After she finished her coffee, Isaias stood up and told Sarah she could start the job on a trial period of one week. He asked her if she was ready to go to his house and begin the job immediately. Sarah smiled so big and showed her excitement so much her arms flew up in the air as she said "Yes!" Isaias laughed a little at her enthusiasm. Sarah told Isaias she was ready to begin right away. The owner walked to the door of his office and held it open as Sarah walked out. He asked Sarah to come with him and they left the hotel in a large car. It looked and smelled new. He drove Sarah to his home.

Isaias' house was just outside of the town center. It sat inside a large compound surrounded by a tall concrete wall. Isaias and Sarah sat in the car and waited for a security guard to open the large metal gate with arrowhead spikes on top pointing skyward. There were two small houses and a large main house inside the groomed dirt and gravel compound. The houses had beautiful stacked stone exterior walls. Isaias parked the car and led Sarah into the main house. The interior of the house amazed Sarah. She had never seen anything so lovely and luxurious. The front room where they entered had a beautiful marble floor and the windows had thick red velvet curtains. The sofa and chairs had dark polished wooden backs and legs and the cushions were plush red velvet, matching the curtains perfectly. Against one wall, there was a dark polished wooden liquor bar with crystal bottles, pitchers, and glasses. On the opposite was dark polished wooden piano matching the backs of the furniture and the bar. Isaias asked Sarah to sit down while he went to get his wife.

Isaias returned in a few minutes pushing his wife in her wheelchair. He introduced his wife, Esther, to Sarah. Isaias wheeled Esther to near the corner of the chair Sarah was sitting in and he sat down in an adjacent chair. Isaias told Esther what Sarah had told him about herself and then let Esther ask questions. Esther asked Sarah if she could keep a house as big as this one clean. Sarah told the story that her uncle's house was not as big as this house, but her uncle demanded that it be perfectly clean all the time. She told Esther she kept it as clean as her uncle liked it, most of the time, plus washing his laundry, cooking his food, feeding the sheep and goats, planting and harvesting from the garden, and anything else he told her to do. Of course, Sarah added, that nothing was satisfactory for her uncle when he was drunk. Sarah spoke with believable certainty although she didn't know where the words came from. The conversation flowed seamlessly. Sarah cannot remember all she said or all they spoke about, and although she knew she told many lies to Esther, she kept asking God for forgiveness. The lies she told were just about her family and her recent circumstances to protect herself. She didn't lie to Esther when she told her how hard she would work and how much she appreciated this opportunity. Somehow, in spite of the lies, Sarah felt the Grace of God surrounding her.

Soon the conversation shifted to talking about Isaias's and Esther's son. Esther talked especially proud of how successful he was. Their son, Daniel, had a large furniture manufacturing and distribution business in Gondor. He employed over 300 workers and sold his furniture throughout central and northern Ethiopia from Addis Ababa to Axum. All the furniture in their home and in their hotel came from Daniel's business. Daniel was 30 years old and the only complaint that Esther had of him was that he had not married or given her grandchildren yet. Isaias laughed and assured her Daniel would marry and give them treasures soon.

Isaias took Esther into another room after asking Sarah to excuse them for a few minutes. They returned to the front room shortly and both were smiling. They told Sarah she had the job, if she still wanted it. Of course Sarah told them yes.

Isaias asked Sarah to follow them back outside as he followed Esther in her chair out the door. Isaias led them to one of the smaller houses behind the main house and told Sarah this is where she would be staying. Sarah went inside and was amazed at the accommodation. The small cottage had a large room with nice bed, desk, television, wardrobe, and dressing table. There was a door at the end of the room that led to a bathroom with a shower/toilet combination. Sarah was overjoyed and could hardly wait to be alone so she could praise God. She thanked Esther and Isaias very much. Esther showed Sarah several white traditional Abyssinian dresses in the wardrobe and told Sarah that she thought they would fit Sarah well. They would be Sarah's to work in. Esther told Sarah to shower and come inside in an hour for orientation. Esther and Isaias had a cook who would prepare dinner later and Sarah could pick her meals up from the kitchen after her chores were finished and eat in her room. Isaias pushed Esther out of the cottage and back across the compound to the main house leaving Sarah alone to shower. As soon as they left, Sarah closed the door and immediately fell on her knees beside the bed and began praising God! God had been so protective of her and wonderful to her. Sarah acknowledged God for all His gifts and was thankful to be so very blessed!

After praying and singing a few praise songs, Sarah noticed a Bible on the desk. She read a few verses from the book of Psalms and prayed another short prayer of thanks to God. Sarah showered and put on one of the white dresses. It fit well, perhaps a little longer than she preferred, with the hem almost touching the floor, but it was very nice and felt clean and good against her skin.

Sarah went back to the main house, knocked on the door, and Esther met her. Esther was good at maneuvering the wheelchair on her own; she told Sarah she just preferred Isaias push her when he is available, "to keep him busy". Isaias had gone back to the hotel now. Esther gave Sarah a chore chart and explained it to her. Then, Esther showed Sarah the entire house and with specific comments on how she wanted everything cleaned, methodology and standards. Esther spent about three hours explaining everything to Sarah, very thoroughly, but very kindly. Sarah continued to beam a smile throughout the afternoon. They were still going through the house, but actually almost finished, when Isaias returned from his day at the hotel. Esther told Sarah to pick her food up in the kitchen and enjoy her dinner. Sarah could pick up her breakfast at 7 A.M. the next morning, wash the dinner and breakfast dishes at 8 A.M., and begin her day cleaning. Sarah went to the kitchen, introduced herself to the chef, picked up her dinner, and went back to the guesthouse. Sarah said grace and thanked God again for all He had done for her. Sarah ate and drank water. The dinner was so delicious and filling. She washed the dishes off a bit in the sink in the bathroom and left them leaning against the wall as she washed her face. Sarah removed the beautiful white dress and hung it up. She lay on the bed with the Bible reading from Isaiah 43; she especially noted verses 2-3:

> "When you pass through the waters, I will be with you; and when you pass through the rivers, they will not sweep over you. When you walk through the fire, you will not be burned; the flames will not set you ablaze. For I am the Lord, your God, the Holy One of Israel, your Savior. I give Egypt for your ransom, Cush (Sudan) and Seba (Ethiopia) in your stead."

Sarah went to her knees and prayed such a long prayer of thanksgiving for all God had brought her through and she sang a few praise songs. Then she walked to the wall, turned off the lights, fell into the soft bed, pulled up the thick blanket, and went into a deep sleep.

Sarah woke up early in the morning, even before the sun was up. She prayed, washed her face, and put on the white dress. She went across to the main house with the dishes from her dinner. The security guard saw Sarah standing by the door; he came and unlocked the door for her. Sarah went into the kitchen where the chef was preparing breakfast. Sarah helped the chef wash and peel some fruit. They talked. He told her how Isaias and Esther were good people to work for and how much he enjoyed his job. He cooked for them at the house and he cooked lunch and dinner at the hotel, too. Sarah ate her breakfast while listening to the chef. His voice was pleasant as he talked about his job and his family. The chef took the breakfast he had prepared for Isaias and Esther into the dining room. Sarah put on an apron and began washing the dinner dishes that had been stacked to the side of the sink and the freshly used dishes from the breakfast preparation. Sarah looked out of the kitchen from time to time to check if they were still eating. She was looking out the window behind the sink as she was washing dishes and saw Isaias get into his car to go to the hotel. The chef rode with him. Sarah went into the dining room and collected the breakfast dishes and washed those, too.

Sarah's day and new job had begun. She finished the dishes and started on her chore chart. The work was time consuming, but not difficult. Sarah tried to be as thorough as possible in her cleaning and sang praise songs softly as she worked.

Esther appreciated Sarah's hard work and complimented her often. Esther and Isaias liked Sarah. Isaias told Esther he could see something special in Sarah. They could see her strength and commitment to doing the best at whatever she attempted, but there was something else about Sarah, a glow, perhaps from confidence, or a deep joy, but it was obvious that she contained something unusual. They didn't know what it was, but when Sarah heard them talking about it, she knew what it was…. It was the confidence and joy in her faith that God was with her.

CHAPTER 13

DANIEL

Esther and Isaias's son, Daniel, came for a visit just after Sarah's first month of working for them. Although Daniel was over ten years older than Sarah, he fell in love with her the first time he talked to her. Daniel had been focusing on his business and not actively looking for a woman to love. He dated a few women, but mostly found he didn't have time to invest in a relationship. His business was too important to him. His business made his parents proud of him, which made him proud of himself. But the real reason he invested more time and effort into his business than he did in any relationship is because Daniel had not found any woman that sparked a desire in him. When Daniel visited his parents and met their new housekeeper, Sarah, his desire was not just sparked; it exploded. He felt like she was everything he had been waiting for. Sarah was beautiful and athletic. She had the facial structure, skin tone, and body build he admired in women; and he found so much more to love when he talked to her. She had a humble confidence that Daniel found so comforting and desirable. This is the woman that he had been waiting for, the woman he wanted. His first visit with his mother and father, and with Sarah, was only a week. After that, however, Daniel found many reasons, and sometimes no reason, to return to Axum, over the next few months, to visit his mother and father, but really to see and talk with Sarah.

Sarah enjoyed working for Esther and Isaias. They were good people and treated her fair. The work was good. It kept her busy; it was consistent. She could take pride in doing a good job with it, and it helped her forget her pains and troubles from the past few months. Her talks and time spent with Daniel really helped Sarah, too. They actually went on a real date the third or fourth time he came to Axum. Daniel took Sarah to a local artist music concert one

Saturday night after she finished her regular chores, except for the evening dinner dishes. Because Esther and Isaias usually ate dinner after 7 P.M., Daniel got permission from his father, and told Sarah it would be ok if Daniel could take Sarah to the concert and they would wash the dishes together when they returned to the house. Of course, washing the dishes together was a great way to end the evening, too.

By the third month of Sarah working for Isaias, Daniel was visiting almost every weekend. It was about this time that Sarah told Daniel the truth about her past and she was still frightened most nights as she would go to sleep that the Eritrean government was still looking for her and someone would come and take her back to Eritrea. Daniel said he would not tell his parents and that he would do anything he could to protect Sarah. When he came to visit during Sarah's fifth month working for his parents, Daniel asked Sarah to marry him. It frightened Sarah to think of doing something legal, signing papers for a magistrate, having to admit the truth to government officials and what they might do to her. Daniel tried to convince Sarah he would go to Addis Ababa, the Ethiopian capital to file refugee status for her first. But Sarah was still afraid.

Sarah worked for Esther and Isaias for a little over six months. Approximately one month after Daniel first asked Sarah to marry him, Daniel convinced Sarah to go to Addis Ababa to file for refugee status. He had called refugee offices himself and was told Sarah would have to go to Addis Ababa herself. They would not get married until after Sarah was a legal refugee. Sarah was still afraid, but with Daniel's persuasion, she agreed to go to Addis Ababa with him. Sarah however, made Daniel promise not to tell his parents, or anyone else, anything until after she had received legal refugee status. Sarah went into the dining room one night, as Esther and Isaias were eating dinner, about a week before her and Daniel had planned to go, and told them she was going to Addis Ababa for a while. It was sad telling them she was leaving and Esther cried asking if they had done anything wrong. Sarah hugged Esther and told her no, they had been very good to her and she appreciated them very much but she had to go to Addis Ababa for family matters. Isaias told Sarah that if she needed anything, he would be happy to help her. Sarah told him she had saved up enough money to take care of herself for a while and how thankful she was for him giving her this job. It was a sad time, but Sarah remembers how relieved she was telling them she was leaving, thinking of getting further away from the border and getting refugee status.

Daniel came that weekend. They went to the airport and flew to Addis Ababa together. Sarah was frightened to be in an airplane. She remembered watching them fly over as a child bombing the villages. It did not seem real at all as she looked out the window to the ground below. It was like a movie, the opposite view as what she saw as a child. She shuddered, cried, and prayed the entire two hours it took to fly to Addis Ababa with Daniel holding her hand the entire way. Sarah's prayers were not just from fear of her first flight and of bad memories; she prayed of her thanksgiving to a gracious God for protecting her and giving her this opportunity to move further away from fears of captivity. Praise God! He is good!

It was a Saturday in May 2005 when Sarah and Daniel went from Axum to Addis Ababa. Sarah was so happy to be away from Axum and the Eritrean border. Addis Ababa was a huge city, sprawling in all directions with taller, more modern buildings than she had ever imagined. Daniel stayed with Sarah in a hotel, in separate rooms, for a little more than a week. They met with Daniel's friend on Monday to begin the refugee application process. The initial paperwork was completed on Tuesday morning, but acceptance and documentation would take an additional week or more of waiting. Sarah told the officials of being chased by the National Security Investigators and escaping across the border, but did not tell them about having been inducted into the Eritrean Army, of her training, or of her hurting or possibly killing a soldier while escaping. She was afraid that would disqualify her from being a refugee and she would be sent back to Eritrea as a criminal. Although Sarah was nervous about holes in her story, they never asked any further questions about her escape from Eritrea. Sarah prayed very intently, every morning, every evening, and every time she closed her eyes before answering questions. The interviews and paperwork went smooth and without any seeming suspicions, by the power of God.

Daniel showed Sarah around Addis Ababa the rest of the week. Daniel was very happy and dreamed of how it would be to be married to Sarah. Sarah, however, began to realize her feelings for Daniel were different than his feelings toward her. And, Sarah knew in her heart, she could never go back to Axum, to being that close to Eritrea.

Daniel paid for the hotel for them both, bought Sarah a cell phone to use, gave Sarah spending money, and paid her hotel bill in advance for two weeks. He told her he would return in two weeks. If her refugee status had been granted by then, they would return to Axum together and start planning their marriage. Until then, Daniel told Sarah that they would talk on the phone every day. Sarah went to the airport with Daniel and told him goodbye. When Daniel said he would see her in two weeks, though, Sarah did not reply. She knew they wouldn't. Daniel flew back to Axum, sad to be leaving the woman he loved, but happy with dreams of their future marriage. Sarah went back to her hotel, happy at being so far from her nightmares of Eritrea, but sad at the thought of hurting Daniel.

Daniel called Sarah every night on the phone. They would talk about any progress in the refugee status; it was moving slowly. Daniel would talk about his dreams of how their wedding would be. Sarah would pretend to agree at some of the details and disagree with things she would not have liked, but never really agreeing or disagreeing about the wedding itself.

Sarah's refugee status was granted on the second Thursday after arriving in Addis Ababa, with just a final paperwork push on the following Monday. The country of Ethiopia granted Sarah asylum and the United Nations High Commission for Refugees (UNHCR) granted Sarah International Refugee status. Sarah requested to be transferred by IOM (the International Organization for Migration, a refugee implementing partner of the United Nations) to a refugee camp in Uganda because of her fears of being in Ethiopia and the perceived hatred of Eritreans by Ethiopians. After facilitating an expedited Ethiopian issued Refugee Travel Document Book (i.e. international passport) for Sarah, IOM would fly her to the camp in Uganda on the following Wednesday. When Daniel called her on Monday night, Sarah first told him of the great news. She told him not to come and get her because they were sending her to Uganda. Sarah told Daniel how grateful she was to him for all his care and love, but she was still confused by all that had happened in the past year and she was not sure if she loved him enough. She could not agree to marry him. Sarah told Daniel they would stay in contact and keep praying for God's will. Daniel was heartbroken. He told Sarah that he loved her and would always be available to help her, but that was the last time they spoke to each other.

CHAPTER 14

UGANDA

It was a sunny day in June 2005 that Sarah stepped out of the United Nations (UN) airplane in Entebbe, Uganda. It had rained earlier in the day, but the clouds had blown away now and a cool breeze off of Lake Victoria next to the Entebbe Airport welcomed Sarah. Sarah remembers standing at the top of the stairs as she exited the plane thinking that the air felt and smelled different than any she had sensed before. She knew that this was the place God had intended for her to be and everything would be good now. Life would be good now and God is great! She said, "Praise God! Amen," perhaps a bit louder than she had intended, but she was conscious not to yell it too loud. She began to sing songs of praise she remembered as she walked down the stairs and entered the airport immigration center. God had truly blessed her. God was indeed good!

IOM had set up a special counter area for the refugees with Uganda Immigration Officers sitting behind the counter. As welcoming as the Uganda air had been, the calming feelings ended with Uganda police and soldiers pushing the refugees, keeping them in line and ensuring none strayed. The Immigration Officers were a bit rude, but stoically took the refugees photos and stamped the refugees' International Travel Documents. The Uganda soldiers escorted the refugees to a large UN truck and supervised the loading. The IOM workers interceded a few times to remind the soldiers to not mistreat the refugees. Sarah began to have flashbacks to being forced into the truck at Dekemhare. How could a blessing from God turn so bad so fast? She hesitated and asked God for help when it came her turn to climb up into the truck. A Uganda soldier swatted her across her lower backside with a wooden baton, to speed her up. An IOM woman began yelling at him and they argued as Sarah climbed up into the truck. Unlike the Eritrean military truck from Dekemhare, this UN truck was covered and there were benches on both sides. The refugees sat on either side leaving plenty of room to stretch their legs in the middle. Sarah sat and said a prayer of praise and asked God to forgive her for the momentary loss of faith. She gave thanks for God's unfailing Grace and began to sing hymns of praise again. Sarah closed her eyes and remembered the Bible scripture Mark 9:24, "Yes, Master, I believe! Help my unbelief!"

As the truck filled up with refugees, Sarah tried to stay close to the rear of the truck. The truck had a thick cover on it and Sarah thought it would protect them from the dust. She wanted to stay near the rear so she could see out. She wound up being the third person from the rear of the truck. She would be able to get fresh air and a good view. As the truck left Entebbe, she saw a sprawling but not over-developed area with residences, restaurants, and small businesses. The road was paved, but traffic was bad and there were several potholes causing bumps and sudden stops. Sarah was so grateful it was still so much better than the truck ride between Dekemhare and Barentu. The truck took them through the capital city of Kampala. The traffic became worse and the truck spent more time stopped than moving forward. However, it was still a pleasurable ride for Sarah. Kampala was much more built up and more modern than what Sarah had imagined… much more than Axum, much more than Asmara, and perhaps even more busy and modern than Addis Ababa. The air was cool and tasted cleaner in her mouth. When the truck finally got through the city of Kampala, they embarked on a road that alternated passing between small villages and forest. Sarah hadn't seen such lush thickness of trees as she saw in these areas. The truck continued into the evening and reached the city of Gulu around a couple hours after sunset, approximately 9 P.M. The truck stopped at a truck stop to refuel. IOM workers and Uganda soldiers watched the refugees as they were allowed to get off the truck, stretch, and the IOM workers gave them bottles of water, plates of beans, and slices of baked bread. The texture of the bread was different than what Sarah was used to, but she enjoyed it…. But she missed injera. The refugees reloaded the truck under the watchful eyes of the Uganda soldiers; the Uganda soldiers were under the watchful eyes of the IOM representatives. They drove for about another hour before arriving at the refugee camp.

Sarah could not see the front of the entrance to the refugee camp then from inside the covered back of the truck, but she was to see it many times in the coming months. The camp was large with a combination of tents and rudimentary thatched roof clay houses. The camp was surrounded by a fence and two strands of razor wire. The road going into the camp had a weighted drop-bar gate with a wooden guard shack and two armed Uganda military guards. There were two Uganda National Police dark blue armored personnel carriers with machine guns and 40 mm cannons parked on either side of the gate. Sarah could see parts of the camp from the back of the truck as they approached the two camp administrative buildings in the center of the camp. These buildings were brick with corrugated tin roofs and were the only two permanent looking buildings in the camp. The camp had several latrines and shower areas with wooden frames and thick army green canvas walls, mostly along the edges of the camp with slit trenches leading under the razor wire to a large ditch on the outside of the camp. There were also trenches along the dirt roads throughout the camp to channel "grey water" sewage and rain run-off. The camp was not attractive or inviting and it had a disgusting odor. Although the camp had more buildings and the refugees were walking freely throughout the camp, the security of the camp reminded Sarah of the training camp at Barentu.

Sarah was a bit frightened at the camp and began second guessing her decision to leave Daniel in Ethiopia to come to Uganda. She could have lived a good life with Daniel. She could have gotten a job and even went to school. Now she would have to work hard at something to scrape by, in a nasty camp surrounded by strangers. Sarah considered all the negatives as the truck stopped and the refugees began to offload. Sarah climbed down from the truck and looked all around. Yes, it was ugly, but she wasn't being beaten; she was far from the dust and threats of Eritrea; she would have the opportunity to do what she wanted to do within the confines of the camp; and, most of all, she knew she would be able to be free from the camp soon. Sarah looked up at the sky and saw the sun coming out from behind some dark clouds—its bright rays radiating out through the lighter wispy clouds. She knew that God would care for her and protect her in this new world and she would have the freedom and better life she dreamed of soon.

The refugees were taken inside one of the camp administration buildings and were instructed to sit down behind long tables where IOM Refugee Camp administrators checked each of the new refugees' papers. They made residential placements for each of the new refugees and offered appointments for counselling and job placement opportunities. They assigned Sarah to a tent with five other girls. They provided Sarah with sheets and a sleeping blanket for the cot, a new pair of pants, two new t-shirts, and a large wrap around cloth. An IOM representative showed Sarah and the other five women to their tent. The tent had a thick plastic sheet as a floor and was bare except for six cots. The IOM representative, a young white woman, was very pleasant, talked kindly and respectfully to the refugee women. Inside the tent, she went around and talked with each woman individually as they spread their sheets on their respective cot. The girl asked Sarah if she had scheduled an appointment. Sarah told her she had not yet but was interested in getting a job as soon as possible. The young woman introduced herself as Cindy and told Sarah she could meet with her the next day at midday. Sarah agreed and they shook hands and laughed a short laugh together. It seemed comfortable to Sarah. After the IOM representative left, Sarah went to her knees beside her cot, asked God to forgive her for her doubts and quick criticism of the camp, and praised God for all He had done for her. God was indeed so very good!

Sarah walked to the Camp Administration buildings at noon the next day and found Cindy. Cindy took Sarah to an empty table and they sat down and discussed what Sarah liked and what she thought she might enjoy doing in the camp. They decided on sewing, and Cindy told Sarah she could set her up in a tent with sewing machines and several other women working as seamstresses. They could teach Sarah how to use the sewing machine and sewing techniques. Cindy said that there was always a lot of business in the camp for the seamstresses; Sarah could stay as busy as she wanted to, work when she wanted to, and make money while providing a needed service for the camp. IOM would provide the thread and material for sheets and clothing when the refugee customers did not provide their own material. Cindy led Sarah out of the administration building and walked her to the sewing tent where she could work. There were three women working inside the sewing tent and an empty table with a sewing machine. Cindy told Sarah that would be her assigned sewing machine to use as much as she wanted. Sarah sat down behind the sewing machine as Cindy introduced her to the other women working there. Sarah felt comfortable and happy. Cindy and Sarah left the sewing tent and walked to the group dining tent and had lunch together. Sarah had never spoken to a white person before and felt very relaxed and happy with her new friend Cindy.

Sarah learned the sewing machine quickly and worked hard. Business was good; everyday so many women would bring in clothes to be repaired or material to make dresses and children's clothes. Sarah was courteous to her clients and soon got a good reputation to where women would come into the tent and ask for Sarah by name. Sarah felt so blessed to have good work, provide such a needed service, and earn relatively good money, too. She sang hymns of praise to God as she worked on the sewing machine and praised God every night for all the miracles He had made in her life.

Sarah became friends with the other ladies working in the sewing tent. Some of the women learned the songs Sarah sang and some would even sing with her sometimes. The ladies in the sewing tent and the women in her sleeping tent were mostly refugees from Sudan or Congo and only spoke Arabic or English. It was difficult for Sarah because she did not speak either. Sarah did not have much English in school; she just remembered the basics. Sarah enjoyed learning English and enjoyed trying to practice the new language. Cindy spoke a little Amharic, similar to Tigrinya, Sarah's language, and she would help Sarah with her English. They would spend time together most evenings teaching Sarah better English and talking about Sarah's experiences.

Cindy came to visit Sarah almost every day and soon they were best friends. Cindy took Sarah to lunch at the refugee camp Administrators' cafeteria often; the refugees were usually not permitted inside except as a special guest of camp administrative personnel. Sarah appreciated the privilege and Cindy's friendship. She felt honored to sit at the table with Cindy and the other camp staff. Although she didn't understand everything they said—she was not used to the fast English they spoke and their different accents—she understood some of it and pretended to understand the rest. Listening to the conversations helped Sarah learn English even more. Most of all, she loved it when they laughed and she would laugh with them. Cindy would sense when Sarah didn't understand something at the lunch table and she would get close to her and explain it, then they would laugh together.

Sarah enjoyed most of her time in the refugee camp. She enjoyed her work, talking and singing praises with the ladies in the sewing tent, and meetings and lunches with Cindy. Time passed quickly. It wasn't as bad as she thought it would be when she first arrived. But the camp was dirty, the roads and alleys between the tents and shacks were dirt, actually mud most of the time because it rained every day; the air was dusty; and sewage drainage ditches rans down the sides of the roads, right in front of the entrances to the shacks and tents.

Internally Displaced Persons (IDP) Camp, (Photo by Tredway)

The camp was heavily littered with plastic and paper trash. There were also piles of fruit and vegetable refuse at the sides of the tents and shelters, rotting and foul smelling. Sometimes the stink throughout the camp was almost intolerable. Only the wind circulating the air made it barely bearable. Children ran and played in the narrow dirt roads and alleys along the sewage drainage ditches and in the refuse piles. Even though there were good UN / IOM / NGO run medical clinics in the camp, most of the children were sick most of the time; their crying day and night echoed through the camp. It rained most mornings and around 3 P.M. every afternoon. The roads were muddy when it rained and for an hour or two after the rain. Then it became so hot when the sun came out, that the roads would dry quick and the wind would blow the dust from the dried dirt roads into everything, in Sarah's hair, in her clothes, red dust on her arms and face. Sarah would have to scrub her face every night to get the dust off. It was different than the light dust in Eritrea that would wash off easy.

Refugee Camp (Photo by Tredway)

Sometimes, mostly at night when she laying her cot, after her prayers, as she tried to go to sleep, listening to the families in the tents around her group sleeping tent, Sarah would miss home so much. She would remember the home with her mother, her sister, and her brothers. Sarah would praise God for what she had and for His protection of her. She was appreciative, but sometimes she would cry herself to sleep.

Sarah stayed in the refugee camp for a little more than two years. Day after day spent walking down the narrow dirt roads between the tents and the tin shacks, between her sleeping tent and the sewing tent. Although she had made a lot of friends, especially her new best friend, Cindy, Sarah knew it was time to go. Sarah had saved up enough money for transportation from the refugee camp in Gulu to Kampala, the capital of Uganda, and for her to spend a couple weeks living in a hostel in the capital city. She had calculated, with advice from Cindy, that it would be enough to eat and live on until she found a job. Cindy warned her, though, that after Sarah signed out of the refugee camp, she would not be able to return to the camp. Sarah would lose her refugee status. Cindy also told her that she could not use her International Travel Document (that the UN had provided her in Addis Ababa) to travel to another country, Sarah could go to the Uganda Immigration Office and apply for

Ugandan residency, Cindy also advised Sarah to go to the Ethiopian Consulate in Kampala as they might be able to assist her in getting an Eritrean Passport. It would not be easy living in a big city starting with little money, no possessions, and no friends. Cindy had talked to some friends of hers in Kampala and found some Eritreans living there. Cindy gave Sarah some contact phone numbers.

Sarah went around the camp the evening before she left and said goodbye to all her friends. Early the next morning, Sarah signed out of the refugee camp. She stood in front of the camp where she had entered two years before. She was grateful for the time she had spent there, the friends she had made, the sewing skills she had learned and practiced, the general safety of the camp, but she was really glad to be moving on to the next chapter of her life.

Cindy gave Sarah a ride into the town of Gulu. They found the tax-park (where buses waited to be filled to travel to their destination). Cindy helped Sarah negotiate the price for the trip. The young ladies hugged and cried for each other. Cindy gave Sarah and envelope as a going away gift, enough money for Sarah to buy a cheap cell phone until she could get a job and save enough money to buy a better one. Sarah cried even more with thanks and praise to God. Sarah gave Cindy one more hug and promised to call her when she arrived in Kampala. Sarah got on the bus and waited as it filled up and left for Kampala.

The bus ride from Gulu to Kampala was bumpy over the poorly maintained paved highway, but it was so much better than the previous long rides Sarah had been on, riding in the back of trucks without seats and choking on dust. The bus was almost completely full, with all seats being occupied and some people even standing in the center aisle. There was a man sitting next to Sarah, pushing against her, but it was ok. Sarah closed her eyes and imagined the better life God had planned for her ahead. Sarah knew that God was with her and joy filled her soul.

It was about 4 P.M. when the bus pulled into the center tax-park in Kampala. The bus driver told Sarah where she could find a cheap hostel in an area of Kampala where a lot of Eritreans stayed. Sarah saw a phone shop and bought a small inexpensive cell phone with the money Cindy had given her. Sarah got on a boda-boda (a motorcycle taxi) and went to the hostel the bus driver had told her. They provided her a small room, one just big enough for a small mattress on the ground and a bucket of water. Sarah went back out to the streets to walk until dark, still amazed at the big modern city of Kampala. She was surprised when she walked by a Habesha (Ethiopian) restaurant. She could hear people inside speaking Amharic and Tigrinya with the typical Ethiopian voice inflections. She felt like she was back in Axum. The restaurant was called the Ethiopian Village. She went inside and sat down at a table. She was overjoyed when a young girl brought her a pitcher of water to wash her hands (a Habesha tradition) and a plate of injera rolls.   Sarah talked with the waitress in Amharic and asked her to sit down with her, but the waitress said she couldn't because she was busy then, but she would come back later. Sarah was just so excited to have someone to talk to in her own language. She ordered a "fasting" (vegetarian) meal, which came quickly. Sarah bowed her head and praised God so passionately for the blessing He had provided her and the food she had been missing for so long. She pinched the bits of vege-tables and sauces with the injera, tasted, and thought she was already in heaven. It was so delicious. The waitress did return to Sarah's table and sat down with her. They talked for about two hours; it was after dark and more people were coming into the restaurant for the Ethiopian evening meal. The waitress, named Elizabeth, introduced Sarah to several of the Habesha's patrons. It was a great evening for Sarah. She went back to her room and called Cindy. Sarah told Cindy about the Ethiopian restaurant and making new friends already. She also assured Cindy she would call the contacts that Cindy had given her. It was nice having Cindy to reach out to, knowing she was still connected to her. She had jumped from place to place so much, losing her connections, her family, her former husband, Yonis, (even for the short time they had been to-gether), the girls in her barracks at the military training center in Barentu, the girls she met at the market in Hiret, her foster family in Axum—Isaias, Esther, and Daniel—her sewing sisters and sleep tent mates at the refugee camp in Gulu, especially Cindy. They had all meant so much to her and had helped her so much. God had been so gracious to provide her with such good friends. And she knew God was beginning her new life here with so many more friends to come. God had protected her so much. Sarah went to her knees with her elbows on the small mattress; she barely had room for her knees between the mattress and the wall; she placed her toes up on the wall. Sarah thanked God giving Him all the praise she could until she fell asleep.

Sarah woke up still in the contorted position she had fallen asleep in while she was praying. She looked up and saw the morning sunlight shining through the spaces between the corrugated tin wall and the corrugated tin roof. Although she realized her back was stiff, she stayed in the position to praise God for a safe night and ask for a good day ahead. Sarah stood up after finishing her prayer and stretched her back. She washed her face in the bucket of water. She lay down briefly on the mattress and stretched out some more while following the rays of sunlight coming through the small holes in the roof and walls, thinking of how God's love provides light for her life and what glories the day holds for her.

Sarah left her room and began walking in the direction of the Ethiopian Village, where she had visited the previous night. On one of the street corners, she found a lady selling "rolex" (Rolled Eggs—an omelet laid out on and wrapped up in a tortilla called a "chipati" like a breakfast burrito). She bought a rolex and sat down on the curb to eat it. When she finished eating, she began calling the contact numbers Cindy had provided to her. She set up some meetings for the day, one at 10 A.M., one at midday, and one at 4 P.M. Sarah found a piece of paper on the curb and borrowed a pen to write the appointments down. She went back to her room and washed herself before going to her first appointment.

Sarah went to those three appointments. One told her they would consider her and call her if they decided to hire her. The other two gave her more contacts that she called and made other appointments for later in the week. She continued to make and go to her appointments with prospective employers including restaurants, hotels, and gas station markets, for the rest of the week. She would interview and schedule more interviews during the day and pray at night. Sarah knew that God was with her and she refused to let her faith and patience die. And God was with Sarah. She received a call back one evening and got a job working at a gas station. She started working in the small market attached to the gas station, stocking the shelves and cleaning. After a few days, one of the other girls working there, Betty, asked Sarah if she wanted to live with her. Sarah had been staying in the small hostel room, with no space to bathe or wash her clothes, and no way to cook for herself. She was very excited to move in with Betty. It was a two-room apartment. The front room had a sofa and a small TV and the bedroom had a double-sized bed. The apartment also had a small kitchen with a sink and a single burner gas stove, and a bathroom with a shower. Betty's apartment was closer to the gas station than the hostel Sarah had been staying in. It was more convenient for Sarah, and her share of the rent would be less expensive than the hostel. She could take nice showers, wash her clothes, and cook her own food.

Betty was a young Ugandan girl. She had moved from a remote village a few months earlier and gotten the job cleaning at the gas station. She did not speak English very well but she was a hard worker. Betty was glad to have someone to share the apartment. The owner of the gas station, a Syrian named Idriss, owned the apartment and only charged Betty half the rent for the first month she worked for him, but the past month, she had to pay full rent. The full rent was too much for her small salary and still buy food and clothes. It would be a comfortable payment with a paying roommate. Sarah slept on the sofa the first few days but then they started sharing the bed. It was big enough for them both. Betty and Sarah became best friends. They shared more than the bed and the apartment. They enjoyed each other's company and conversation, and, most importantly, they shared a deep faith in God. They shared their experiences of God's love in their lives, and prayed together, kneeling beside each other thanking God for all His blessings before going to sleep each night.

Sarah worked hard at the gas station market, cleaning the floors, cleaning the bathrooms, and stocking the shelves. She also unloaded trucks when they brought supplies and anything else she was asked to do. She volunteered to do things she saw that needed done even if she wasn't asked. She was always friendly to the other workers and to customers. Sarah's English improved significantly and she soon became one of the owner's favorite employees. After a month, Sarah began filling in for the cash register attendants, first just when they had to go to the bathroom or run short errands for the owner, Idriss. After another couple weeks, Idriss put Sarah as a full-time cash register attendant. She was glad for the easier work and more interface with customers, but she missed walking around and doing different things a bit. She also got a pay raise, which she really appreciated.

Life was good for Sarah. Betty was a great friend and roommate. Sarah was making many other new friends. Her job was good. She was earning enough money to eat well and buy nice clothes. She was even able to go out to eat and meet friends once or twice a week.

Sarah called Cindy at least once a week. It was nice to talk with her and Sarah was proud to tell her how good she was doing in Kampala. Cindy always complimented Sarah on her success and how good her English was becoming.

Cindy also gossiped a bit about the girls Sarah remembered from the refugee camp in Gulu… but nice things, nothing bad. The phone calls with Cindy meant a lot to Sarah. And it was great when Cindy came to Kampala for a weekend once and they went to eat together. Sarah even convinced Cindy to let Sarah pay for the meal. That really made Sarah happy that she could pay for the meal, at least to show some appreciation to Cindy for all the nice things she had done for her.

Sarah also began to develop strong friendships with Eritreans she met. The Eritrean community was actually quite large and very close in Kampala. They would meet often at a Habisha restaurant, usually the Ethiopian Village. Whenever Sarah would meet Eritrean friends for dinner or game night at some of their homes, she would think about her family. She sent messages back with some Eritreans that were able to travel to Asmara, hoping that they might be able to contact her parents. Soon after Sarah's second year in Kampala, an Eritrean man returned to Uganda from Asmara saying that he had a friend that knew Sarah's family and he gave Sarah a contact phone number. Sarah didn't call right away; she was too nervous and regretful. Sarah wanted to ask for her family's forgiveness for all the bad she felt she had done to them and for any disgrace she had brought them. She finally gathered her inner strength and called the contact. The man she called told her he knew her family; he told Sarah her father had died, but her mother was still alive and doing ok. He gave Sarah the phone number of her mother, Semhar. Sarah was crushed that her father had died and she cried for days. Her friends and coworkers sympathized with Sarah and tried to help, but the guilt of thinking it was her fault for not seeing him before he passed was too much. Sarah prayed that Isaac was in a better place, in glory at the feet of God.

Sarah waited a little more than a week before she had to courage to call her mother. When she finally heard her mother's voice, she assured Semhar that it was actually Sarah and she was alive and well. They both cried. Through the tears, Sarah apologized for causing all the trouble she had caused the family and asked for forgiveness. At the end of the conversation, Sarah felt Semhar's love, but was not sure if she had been forgiven. The next week, when Sarah called Semhar again, Semhar told her she had told her brothers Sarah was alive, but they did not want to know about her. Sarah knew forgiveness would take a long time.

Sarah was not just feeling guilty of leaving her family, but also deserting the military and maybe even killing someone. Of course she could never tell even her closest friends of that. She was still afraid that she could be taken back to Eritrea and executed for that.

Betty and another friend of Sarah's told her forgiveness would have to begin from inside. Sarah would have to forgive herself first, for healing to begin. If her family forgave her one day, that would be great and be a blessed day. But, if not, Sarah had to know that she did what she had to do to survive and she had to be justified with herself before she could expect her family to forgive her. Sarah prayed with her friends about it; they all cried. Sarah cried herself to sleep while praying by herself that night. God came to Sarah that night, in her dreams: Sarah was with her father. She was standing at the gates to Heaven looking in at her father on the other side. Her father could walk and looked completely strong and healthy. He came to Sarah and put his arms around her, crying with her. Isaac told Sarah that he forgave her; actually, he said there was nothing to forgive. Then a warm cloud circled them both. Sarah felt the presence of God in the cloud pressing her and her father together. Isaac whispered in Sarah's ear that he loved her; she was still his precious little girl. Then the voice of God so loud surrounding them, yet so soft and tender, told Sarah she was loved and forgiven. God had always been with her and He would always be with her. Sarah woke up and knew she was loved and forgiven by the ones that mattered most… her earthly father and her Heavenly Father. Amen!

Sarah continued to work hard at the gas station. She ran the register long hours and still helped out unloading trucks and stocking shelves when no customers were around and after closing. The owner's appreciation of Sarah grew. After six months, when the previous finance bookkeeper quit for a better job, Idriss taught Sarah how to do daily cash count-outs and manage the weekly financial books. Sarah still ran the cash register during the days and evenings, but now she also stayed at work later to count the till and log cash and receipts. She also balanced the financial books on Saturday nights and Sundays. Idriss understood, although he was Muslim, that Sarah had to be free to go to church services on Sunday morning. She worked fulltime on Sundays the first few weeks working at the gas station, then she requested and was allowed for Sundays to be her day off. Now, he still allowed Sarah to have Sunday mornings and early afternoons off, but she would come in at 2 P.M. and balance the books, usually just taking until about 5 P.M. Then Sarah would go to another evening church service at 6 P.M.

Betty would go to the morning and evening church services with Sarah and they remained good friends even though Sarah was promoted from cleaning and stocking to cash register attendant and then to bookkeeper. Betty stayed in the cleaner role throughout, mostly because of her limited English. She understood English good enough, but was shy to speak it much. Sarah worked with her at night, but Betty was still slow to gain confidence with it. After Sarah had lived with Betty for a little more than a year, Betty decided to quit the gas station and move out of the apartment to go back to her home village. Sarah continued to live in the apartment; the owner gave her a discount on rent after Betty left, until Sarah arranged for another girl to live with her. It took almost two months to find someone. Sarah finally found an Eritrean girl, Abeba (Flower), that worked in a hotel, to join her in the apartment. Like with Betty, Sarah became very close to Abeba. Sarah was even Abeba's maid of honor at her wedding a couple years later.

Sarah worked for Idriss at the gas station for three more years, a little over four years total. She felt so blessed to have worked there steady, so long and had saved money and lived comfortably. Sarah became able to send money to her mother, through friends travelling to Eritrea. It wasn't much, but Sarah wanted to help her family when she could. Sarah would call her mother to confirm her receipt of the money, but never received a thank you. Semhar would never say much or talk about her family at all. The call would always be flat and cold and Sarah would always cry after hanging up. Sarah still loved her mother, sister, and brothers very much. She prayed that they could one day be together again and she could show them her love.

After four years at the gas station, Sarah was offered a job as bookkeeper and personnel manager of a large mechanic and metal fabrication shop owned by a friend of Idriss. The new position actually offered Sarah almost twice the salary, and although Idriss regretted losing Sarah, he owed his friend a favor and was glad to see Sarah get a better paying job. Sarah worked at the mechanic shop for three years. She stayed living in the apartment with Abeba during those three years, making good money and good friends. Sarah spent almost seven years in Kampala and a total of nine years in Uganda. It had been nine good, God-blessed years since she left Eritrea, and Sarah praised God every night for each day.

During the early years Sarah had been in Kampala, she did not date. She had developed casual friendships with many men, mostly Eritreans, Ethiopians, and some Ugandans. She spent most of her free evenings at the Habesha Ethiopian Restaurant, drinking soda or white wine with her friends. She went out with a young Ethiopian man once, sometime during her third year of living in Kampala; she remembers it was before she shifted jobs to the mechanic shop. But Sarah was uncomfortable and even frightened during the entire evening with him; perhaps she might tell him too much about her past; perhaps he would turn her in; perhaps he would tell someone, another Ethiopian or an Eritrean that could lead to her being deported back to Eritrea for punishment. She decided she could never go out with another Ethiopian or Eritrean. She also went out twice with Ugandan men. Sarah did not like the way they talked to her or the way they treated her. Unlike her male Ugandan friends, the men she went out with treated her rude. Perhaps she was oversensitive because she had seen how several of her friends had been treated by Ugandan men. Stories from her friends showed most Ugandan men talked too demeaning to women and were abusive to them. These men only wanted sex from the relationship. They would dump their woman after a short time after having sex a few times, and would find other women to have sex with, sometimes even while previous relationships were ongoing. It was all she could think of when she was out with them. Whether it was the Ugandan men's actual treatment of her or just her perception of their treatment, Sarah felt uncomfortable and underappreciated when she was out with them. She would rather just hang out with her friends.

In 2010, when she was 25 years old, Sarah began to think that life and love were passing her by. She knew God loved her and she was thankful for all God had done for her. But, she felt like she needed physical love from a man. Her friends all talked about their relationships, good and bad. Sarah felt left out and wanted a deep relationship with a man. Even though had been married, she was still a virgin. She was only 16 when she got married, and it was an arranged utilitarian marriage with no real love. They had planned on having sex after Sarah turned 18 years old, but Yonis divorced her before then. Sarah often wondered what it would feel like to really be in love and to make love to a man. She also often remembered the warm feelings she had when she was with Daniel. She wondered if she should have stayed with him. But she knew, for her sanity, she needed to get out of Ethiopia and she praised God for bringing her to Uganda.

There was also a devastating event in Uganda during July 2010. During the 2010 World Cup Football (Soccer) Championship match, the Al-Shabaab terrorist group from Somalia detonated bombs in Kampala, Uganda. Three actual bombs, one in a restaurant on one side of town and two other bombs in a sports club on the other side of Kampala. 74 people were killed in the bombing attacks including 62 Ugandans. It was especially horrific for the Ethiopian and Eritrean community, because the first bomb, going off during the half-time of the championship soccer match, approximately 10:15 P.M., was at the Ethiopian Village Restaurant. The bombing at the restaurant alone killed 15 people, including six Eritreans and one Ethiopian, and injured over 30 others.

Ethiopian Village Restaurant in Kampala, Uganda after the 2010 terrorist bombing. Photo courtesy of Fox News Archives.

a57.foxnews.com/a57.foxnews.com/static.foxnews.com/foxnews.com/content/uploads/2018/09/640/320/1862/1048/uganda_village_071210.jpg?ve=1&tl=1?ve=1&tl=1

The Ethiopian Village was the restaurant Sarah had gone to her first night in Kampala, three years before. It is where she went so often with her friends. Sarah and some of her friends had actually walked to the Ethiopian Village earlier that evening, but found it too busy, so many people there to watch the game, over crowed and too noisy, so they had gone to a smaller Habesha nearby. Sarah was already back home before the explosion. But she heard about it the next day and was devastated. She even knew some of the ones killed. Sarah was so shocked that this could happen in her new home country. Uganda had been so peaceful since she had been there. She cried and prayed so much for several days. It even scared her to think that she could have been in the

Ethiopian Village eating when the bomb went off. She or one of her friends could have been injured or died. Even though the tragedy grieved her so much, she still praised God for bringing her to Uganda and for keeping her safe.

Sarah remained cautious when it came to men. She continued to refuse to go out with Ugandan men because of how she had seen them treat her friends. And Sarah would not date Eritrean or Ethiopian men because of her fear of them betraying her to the Eritrean government. Sarah met a few Kenyan men and a couple Congolese men she thought were attractive, but she found excuses to not go out with them either.

CHAPTER 15

MUZUNGU

One Sunday afternoon after church, about two years after the bombing, Sarah and a Ugandan friend named Patience, who had gone to Church with her, were sitting at a roadside café drinking coffee. A white man was sitting near them (Patience called him a "Muzungu"—Swahili for "Stranger," actually more common now to mean "White Man," or what Sarah called "Ferengi"— the same as Muzungu in the Ethiopian Amharic language). He kept looking at Sarah and smiling at her. Sarah pretended not to notice him and she acted shy. But he kept looking and probably saw her looking back at him a couple times. Sarah and her friend giggled about it, and Patience told Sarah it looked like the Muzungu liked her.

The man finally walked over to Sarah's table with two large Danish pastries he had ordered. He gave the pastries to Sarah and introduced himself as Eric. Sarah told him her name as she handed one of the Danishes to Patience. Eric asked Sarah if he could call her. Sarah first said, "No!" as sternly as she could, but then her friend pinched her arm and they started laughing. Even Eric laughed. So, Sarah said, "Well, maybe."

Eric asked again, with a childish "Please…?" He was handsome and looked so cute begging. Sarah could not refuse any longer. She gave Eric her phone number. He thanked the ladies and went back to his table. He placed money for his bill in the bill holder and left. Eric looked over his shoulder smiling at Sarah as he walked away.

Sarah and Patience giggled and talked about Eric while eating their Danish pastries and finishing their tea. Sarah asked Patience why she thought the man was interested in her. Patience told her it was because Sarah was so beautiful. But Sarah said she didn't think so, maybe the man had something else on his mind. Maybe he just wanted sex like Ugandan men. Patience told Sarah she didn't think so. "Muzungus do want sex, but they know how to treat women better than Ugandan men. Go out with him and you will see!"

Eric called Sarah that night and they talked for over an hour. Eric told Sarah about his job with the United Nations Development Program (UNDP) helping dig wells in remote villages in Uganda. He sounded nice and honest. He asked Sarah if they could go out on a date the next night… maybe out to eat and to a movie. Sarah told him she worked hard and was mostly tired at night. She refused the offer for the date that first night. Eric began calling and asking every night. Sarah continued to refuse night after night. She wasn't sure why she refused; maybe she was just shy, and perhaps a little afraid. After a few days, Sarah told Eric where she worked and what time she usually got off. Eric began to show up at the mechanic shop where she worked when it was time for her to get off. He would wait until Sarah got off work and walk her home. He was always kind and respectful to her, and most times he would bring her candy that they shared on the walk back to her place.

She enjoyed her walks after work with Eric. He was nice and she enjoyed his different cultural perspectives… He was so different than the other men that usually asked her out and even from the men she had as friends. He was a South African (white) and had a strange accent and tone to his voice. He was very funny, and Sarah liked his sense of humor, even though she didn't understand it sometimes. They talked about a lot of subjects. Sarah enjoyed learning from Eric facts about other countries, his opinions on world issues, and especially on religion. Sarah was happy that Eric was a Christian and he knew a lot about the Bible. They would talk about the meanings of different Bible stories and the parables that Jesus told. It was very refreshing and stimulating for Sarah.

Eric was very persistent. Sarah liked that Eric did not give up easily and she thought his persistence must mean he was really serious about wanting her. After two weeks of walking her home every night, Sarah gave in and accepted his nightly offer of a meal and a movie for the following Saturday night.

Sarah began going out with Eric to a restaurant and sometimes to a movie every Saturday night. Eric continued to walk Sarah home from work every evening. And Eric started going to Church with Sarah on Sunday mornings. Sarah had been going to an Ethiopian Orthodox Church where the service was in Amharic. Because Eric could not speak Amharic and he would not understand the service customs, Sarah took Eric to another church she had been to with Ugandan friends before, Kampala Pentecostal Church (KPC), where they spoke English. They both enjoyed the services at KPC. Sarah really enjoyed the praise songs they sang at KPC better than the Ethiopian Orthodox Church. Sarah could really feel the Holy Spirit moving through her at KPC. She had mostly liked the Ethiopian Orthodox Church because it reminded her of good times of her younger days with her family. She missed her family so much and prayed for them every morning and every night.

Sarah told Eric about her family. She told him she had been forced to leave Eritrea because of military conscription. However, she never told him the full reason why or how she left. Eric was kind in understanding about Sarah missing her family and began giving her money to send to them.

Sarah felt warm and safe when she was with Eric. She appreciated his caring for her and her family. She was grateful for his Christian background and that he was working for an organization that helped so many desperate people. Sarah prayed every night for God to direct her on how to proceed with Eric. She knew that it was time to start a family and felt like Eric would be a good husband and father.

After a month of dating, Eric began asking Sarah to spend the night with her. They had not had sex, and Sarah knew Eric was being very patient with her, but she still told him no, using her roommate as the excuse. But Eric continued asking. One night, about two more months later, Abeba, Sarah's roommate, was staying with another friend. So, after Eric kissed Sarah good night at the gate to her apartment complex, he asked her if he could spend the night, like he always did, and began to turn and walk away, anticipating her typical "no" answer...Sarah grabbed his arm, turned him back around, looked into his eyes and saw his passion. She had to tell him yes! Eric couldn't believe it. He asked if Sarah was sure as he kissed her. Sarah said yes!

Sarah and Eric slept together that night. Sarah was so amazed at how wonderful Eric made her feel. Especially that first time, her first time. Eric was gentle with her but still so passionate and made Sarah feel so loved. Eric began spending other nights with Sarah, every time Abeba spent the night at friends. Eric even booked a hotel room sometimes so Sarah could spend the night with him when Abeba was at their apartment.

Sarah and Eric dated for almost six months when Sarah discovered she was pregnant. Sarah had only slept with Eric less than ten times when she found out she was going to have his baby. Eric was the only man Sarah had made love to, but she knew he was the one she loved and she wanted to spend the rest of her life with him. Although Sarah felt guilty for having sex and getting pregnant outside of God's ordained marriage, she was so thankful to God that Eric was going to be the father of her baby.

Sarah and Eric got married when she was a little more than five months pregnant and just beginning to show. It was a small Uganda civil marriage with only Abeba, plus another of Sarah's closest Uganda girlfriends, and one of Eric's UNDP work colleagues as witnesses. They continued to live separately because Eric said he had to maintain his room in the United Nations compound with UN curfew rules and Sarah couldn't stay there with him. Sarah continued to stay with Abeba. After the wedding, nothing really changed, except Sarah was happier knowing she was married and she and her baby would be taken care of.

About six weeks later, just as Sarah was entering her third trimester of her pregnancy, Eric lost his job with the UNDP. Eric was only given one week to organize for his return to his home country (South Africa). Without his UN work credentials, Eric could not stay in Uganda. Eric had talked to Sarah many times before about one day taking Sarah to South Africa, but this came up very unexpected and a lot of steps had to be taken in less than a week.

Luckily, or perhaps prayerfully, Sarah had thought ahead and had gone to the Eritrean Consulate a few days after her and Eric had gotten married to see if she could get an Eritrean passport. Sarah told the consulate secretary that she had been born in Eritrea but her parents had died when she was a young girl, her village had been destroyed in the war, and her aunt had taken her to Axum, Ethiopia to escape the bombings. Sarah further told the secretary that her aunt died a few years later in Axum and Sarah had been deported by the government of Ethiopia and she was sent to the refugee camp in Gulu, Uganda. After she turned 21 years old, she left the refugee camp in Gulu and came to Kampala. Sarah was given an interview with an Eritrean consular officer and, although she was very afraid, she repeated the same story she had told the secretary. The consular officer listened to Sarah's story very intently and then told Sarah to wait as he left her alone in a small conference room. Sarah heard the officer lock the door when he left. Sarah bowed her head and prayed quietly for God to forgive her for lying and to grant a passport so she could be with her husband if they ever left Uganda. She did not know then that day would come so soon. She thought about her life and all the bad things she had done and how God had always helped her when she needed help. She had done so many bad things as a young girl; she had run away from her family; she had run away from her country and obligations; she had lied; she had stolen; maybe she had even killed a man; and she had had sex with a man and gotten pregnant without first having God Bless their union in legal marriage or with the blessing of the Church. Sarah had faith that God was capable of forgiving her and performing any miracle. Her life had shown her that over and over again. What she did not have faith in was if she deserved His divine intervention. Sarah prayed so hard for God to forgive her and give her a chance to be a good wife and a good mother. The consular officer was gone for a long time… it seemed so long to Sarah. Sarah began to list and give thanks for each of the times she knew God had saved her before. God is indeed so very good! Sarah looked up as the door unlocked and opened. The consular officer came back into the small room and handed Sarah the passport application forms. He told her he would approve her passport, but told her that he was putting a special note in her immigrations file that because she had sought refuge in another country, she could never travel to Eritrea. He helped Sarah fill out the forms, took her passport photo, and told her to come back in one week to pick up the passport. God was good! God is good! All the time!

A week later, just a few days before Eric was scheduled to leave for South Africa, Sarah received a call from the Eritrean Consulate to pick up her passport. She went immediately and signed for it. Sarah left the Eritrean Consulate a very pleased, happy woman, singing praises to God all the way to her apartment. She had a passport and would be able to travel with her husband to his home in South Africa. She would have her baby in a clean safe environment with good medical care. Sarah and her baby would be loved and cared for. As she walked away, a quick thought hurt her to know she would never be allowed to go back to her home country of Eritrea and maybe never to have the opportunity to see any of her family again. But, she thought further, perhaps, some of her family could be able to come and see her one day. She prayed as she continued to walk and convinced herself not returning to Eritrea was actually a good thing. Eritrea had not been kind to her and God had provided a new life for her in Uganda, and now, moving with her new husband to a new exciting chapter in her life in South Africa. God is truly a great and loving Father!

CHAPTER 16
SOUTH AFRICA

Sarah flew with Eric to Johannesburg, South Africa in April 2014. It was so much bigger than Kampala. Everything seemed bigger and everything was cleaner. Eric rented a car and drove Sarah from the International Airport in Johannesburg to his family's goat ranch in Rustenburg of northwest South Africa. The drive was very nice. After leaving the area surrounding the airport with a few traffic jams, they were on a smooth open highway. It was so unlike the roads Sarah had seen in Uganda. The roads were well maintained and relatively garbage free on either side of the highway. Eric drove west from the airport. First, a ring road around the southwest side of Johannesburg, heavily congested with road exits leading to shopping centers and other business. Eric turned off the ring road onto a highway. The first few miles along the highway, Sarah saw a few industrial complexes and gravel pits, then just clean open countryside alternating between areas with grass and small bushes and other areas of evenly spaced medium height trees. It was a very relaxing drive of only a couple of hours before the highway ended at a three-way junction with a larger four-lane highway. The junction was adjacent to a large lake. Eric had been mostly quiet during the drive, until he saw the lake approaching. He told Sarah they were close to his parents' house and ranch and they would be there soon, but he wanted to stop at a friend's house before they went on further.

Eric turned right at the highway junction and stayed on the big road for a few miles then turned off onto a much narrower road. The smaller road was still paved but had a rougher finish. Sarah could feel and hear the difference as the tires roared louder than before. The smaller road led to a housing area. The houses were all single story, very similar in size and shape to each other, all simple three-bedroom ranch houses, but Sarah was very impressed. She especially liked the flower gardens in front of most of the houses. Sarah imagined sitting on the porch of her and Eric's house, watching their child play in the front yard as she smells the wind drift of the flower's lovely scent.

Eric pulled the rental car into one of the lovely houses' driveway and honked the horn. Eric told Sarah to stay in the car and he would only be a short while. As Eric got out of the car, his friend came out the front door of the house and excitedly greeted him. They hugged and laughed for a couple of minutes on the front porch of the house, and spoke loud with childlike excitement to each other. Sarah could hear them even inside the car, but they were speaking in Afrikaans, a South African language Sarah had not heard before and could not understand. After a few minutes of chatting, his friend exaggeratedly pulled Eric into the house. Sarah stayed in the car alone for what seemed like a very long time, until she fell asleep.

When Eric came out, he and his friend were singing loud in Afrikaans. It startled Sarah and woke her up. The sun had gone down and the area was lit with a glow from Eric's friend's house and the several other houses lined up on both sides of the small street. Eric got into the car without saying anything to Sarah. He started the car and backed out of the short driveway. As he turned onto the neighborhood street, he began yelling at Sarah saying if it was not for her being there, he could have spent the night at his friend's house and had a good time catching up with him. Sarah didn't know what to say. She had never heard Eric talk like this before. He was evidently drunk and seemed extremely genuinely angry with her for inconveniencing him from having a good time with his friend, even though he had been with him leaving her alone in the car for a couple hours. Sarah just turned to the window and looked out, first the houses, then the long roughly paved road with trees on either side, then they turned back onto the four-lane highway. As Sarah looked out the window, Eric continued to yell. He had now started yelling in Afrikaans and she couldn't even understand what he was yelling about. Sarah prayed that Eric would not hit her. She was afraid; although Eric had never hit her before, she had never seen him drunk or angry before. All she could do was pray and look out the window. By the time they turned onto the big highway, Eric had stopped yelling and just looked ahead as he drove into the darkness. Eric drove back past the lake and continued on for about 30 minutes in silence before turning off the highway onto another roughly paved road. Eric told Sarah that his parents' ranch was on this road, only about five minutes further. This road was darker still. The night was cloudy, and Sarah could not even see the moon. Sarah thought about the darkness of the road and wondered what was along this dark path. It was as dark as she could ever remember a night being. Sarah continued to pray as Eric drove down the rough road and finally turned off onto a dirt road leading up to a large house.

Eric parked the rental car and went into the house alone, leaving Sarah sitting alone, again. He did not say anything to Sarah, just opened the door and walked away as she watched. Sarah didn't know what to do or how long she should sit in the car. After about 30 minutes, Eric came back to the car. She was surprised he came back outside alone. She wondered why his parents or any of his family members had not come outside with him. Eric opened Sarah's door and told her they could take their luggage to the back of the house. Eric had a large hard-sided suitcase and a large soft-sided duffel bag. He carried one bag in each hand by their handles. Sarah only had one small suitcase and she picked it from the back of the car and followed behind Eric. He led her around the side of the house. Eric was moving fast, but Sarah walked slow and cautiously in the darkness. When they arrived to the back of the house, Sarah saw the light coming from the back door of the main house spilling out across a brick paved courtyard. On the opposite side of the courtyard was a small outbuilding in the dark. Eric dropped his bags by the back door. He told Sarah to follow him to the door of the outbuilding. Eric opened the door of the small house, turned on the inside light, and walked inside in front of Sarah. The door opened into a small sitting room with a single over-stuffed double-seated sofa, a long knee-high table against the back wall with a small television sitting on it, and an eating table with two chairs. On the near side of the room, to the right of entering the door was a wall with a pass-through bar looking into the kitchen. A narrow passage break in the wall led into the small kitchen. The kitchen had a counter with a small sink for washing dishes, a dish rack with a couple plates, a bowl, and some eating utensils. There was a waist-high refrigerator and a two-burner stove. On the other side of the sitting room was a closed door.

Eric turned the TV on for Sarah and told her to put down her suitcase and relax for a while; he said he would be back soon. Eric went out the door, walked across the courtyard to the main house backdoor, took his bags inside, and closed the door.

Sarah didn't understand. She was still upset and feeling lost from Eric leaving her to go into his friend's house without her. That made her feel low and lonely, but she somehow understood. She knew Eric had missed his friends after being in Uganda for so long; he just wanted to spend some time catching up with them, having a little to drink with them, laughing with them. Perhaps he was not prepared to introduce his wife to them yet. But this was his family. Why didn't Eric take her into the main house and introduce her to his mother and father? Why did he leave her alone in this small outbuilding… a maid's quarters? Why did he take his bags into the main house and leave her alone?

Sarah turned the TV off, stood in front of the small sofa, and went to her knees. Sarah prayed. Sarah thanked God for all the times He had cared for her; for bringing her safely from Eritrea; for taking care of her in Ethiopia and Uganda; for her health and strength; for the precious life growing inside her; for all the prayers He had answered for her and all the times God had helped her. Then Sarah asked God to help her again; to give her peace, love, and happiness with her husband in this new land; for understanding and patience. She began to cry, but only for a few minutes; silence; then a warm calm settled on her. She had felt this peace from God many times before. She knew God was with her and her unborn baby.

Sarah thanked God again and got to her feet. She looked around. This would not be a bad little house for her, Eric, and their child to begin life together in. Sarah sat on the sofa—it was soft. She went to the kitchen—it was as nice as what she had in her apartment in Uganda. The TV was ok. Sarah went to the door on the far side of the sitting room. It opened into a small bedroom with a double bed and a wardrobe. There was another door on the side of the bedroom that went to a small bathroom with a shower, sink, and sit-down toilet. Everything was nice. Now, she just needed understanding.

The bed was stripped down bare. The sheets and a blanket were folded up piled on the foot of the bed. Sarah felt too tired to make the bed. She thought she would be more motivated to make the bed after Eric came back. Sarah went back to the sitting room, turned the TV back on, sat on the sofa, and waited. She watched the end of one TV show and the news came on. They spoke in both English and Afrikaans. With their fast English accent, Sarah only understood half of the English and none of the Afrikaans. It was too difficult to follow what they were saying, especially as tired as she was. Her mind was clouded and her eyes began closing. She fell asleep.

Sarah woke up to the sound of the door opening. Eric was coming into the small guesthouse. Sarah could see it was morning with the sunlight flooding in through the door silhouetting Eric's body. She realized she had her legs pulled up tight to her extremely large, fully round, pregnant belly, her knees on each side as she sat on the sofa and immediately put her feet down to the floor sending a visual invitation for Eric to sit next to her. Eric walked to Sarah, but didn't sit down. He said, "We have to talk!"

A dread filled Sarah, like the darkness coming down the road to this ranch and the darkness that engulfed her walking around the main house the previous night.

Eric told Sarah he had not previously told his parents that they had gotten married. Actually, Eric had not told his parents about Sarah at all. He told her that his parents were good Christian people, but they had very strong negative thoughts about mixed marriages. They would consider Sarah as black even though she was lighter skinned then many South African whites. They would not accept their marriage soon. He assured Sarah that he was sure they would accept her after they got to know her, and especially after the baby was born. He knew they would be so happy to have a grandchild. They would have to accept their grandchild's mother. Eric explained to Sarah that he wanted to tell his parents that they had already gotten married; he went into the house to tell them, but he had gotten too drunk and could not find the right time or the right words to tell them. Eric had told his parents he was bringing a girl-friend back home with him. They had told him she could stay in the guest-house in the back. They were proper people and did not want any premarital sex in their house. So, until Eric could find the right way and time to tell them they were married, Sarah would have to stay in the guesthouse. Eric assured her he would be looking for a job and find their own place to live soon.

Eric told Sarah he was going back in the house for breakfast and he would bring her some food back. Eric turned and went back out the door closing it on his way out. Sarah was shocked! She did not know what to say and was even too embarrassed, shocked, and ashamed to say anything while Eric had been talking. She brought her knees back up around her womb and held her legs tight. Her mind was numb… she could not think. She doesn't remember how long she sat there like that until her mind started thinking again. Then thoughts came fast, too fast to capture—Should she run away? Should she just be a good girl and accept their way? Perhaps they would accept her soon? What will happen when the baby is born? Why wasn't Eric defending her and taking care of her properly? Why did he even bring her here? No answers came to any of these questions. She was lost, again. Sarah cried.

CHAPTER 17

WITH GOD'S STRENGTH

After some time, Sarah realized she was stronger than she was acting now. And Sarah knew God was stronger than these circumstances. God was, always had been, and would continue to always be with her. She went to her knees as she had the night before and prayed for God to give her strength, wisdom, patience, and understanding. Sarah thanked God for all He had brought her through. She started thinking of all the specific times as images flooded her mind and thanked God for each of them. She remembered how each time God had brought her through the dark valleys bringing her so many victories. Without the low points in her life, she would not recognize and appreciate the mountaintops at the end. Sarah began singing the Andre Crouch song "Through it All."

> I thank God for the mountains,
> and I thank Him for the valleys,
> I thank Him for the storms He brought me through.
>
> For if I'd never had a problem,
> I wouldn't know God could solve them,
> I'd never know what faith in God could do.
>
> Through it all,
> Through it all,
> I've learned to trust in Jesus.
> I've learned to trust in God.
> Through it all,

Through it all,
I've learned to depend upon His Word!

"Through It All "Lyrics. Lyrics.com.
STANDS4 LLC, 2021
https:www.lyrics.com/lyric/847594/Andra%C3%A9+Crouch

Sarah picked up her suitcase from where she had left it by the door the night before and took it into the bedroom. She set the suitcase on the bed and opened it. She looked down at the clothes in the bag and told herself she had to be brave. She would not let people defeat her when she knew God was with her. Sarah took out some clean clothes and went to the bathroom to shower. As she showered, Sarah kept praying and singing. When she finished showering, as she was drying off, she looked at her reflection in a small mirror on the wall.

Sarah said a Bible verse she remembered; she said it out loud to her reflection in the mirror: "If God is for us, who can stand against us!" (Romans 8:31)

Sarah said it again, louder, "If God is for us, who can stand against us!" and a third time, even louder, "If God is for us, who can stand against us!"

Sarah believed it! She knew God had been with her through all her troubles and God would not leave her alone now. God would provide a good life for her and her baby.

Sarah went back to her suitcase and found a Bible she had brought from Uganda. She took the Bible back to the sofa in the front room and began reading from the book of 1 Samuel. Sarah read the story of Hannah and how she cried in the Temple and prayed silently but so intently to God, quietly, moving her lips with the words but not voicing the tones, until Eli the priest came to her, thinking she was drunk and scolded her for coming into the House of God after drinking so much. Hannah explained to Eli that she had not been drinking, she was merely heartbroken and only wanted a son and to give her son a good life. The story made Sarah smile… almost laugh when she thought about how Eli assumed the worst of Hannah, scolding her for drinking when she had really only been praying. Sarah read further how God had answered Hannah's prayers by giving her a son, a son that grew to be the Chief Prophet for King Saul, the first King of Israel, and who would eventually anoint the great King David. How wonderful it is to think that the same God is hearing our prayers. God is faithful to us all.

Sarah went back to her suitcase and put the rest of the few clothes she had into the bedroom wardrobe. She went back to the sofa and watched television for a while and then read her Bible for some time. She went to the door a few times and looked out at the large house across the way and wondered where Eric could be. Although she knew God was with her and everything would be ok, she still hurt thinking her husband could desert her like this.

Eric returned after a few hours with a plate of cold fried eggs, a couple pieces of bread, a banana, and a cup of milk. He set the plate and the cup down on the dinner table and pulled a chair out so Sarah could sit down. Sarah walked over from the sofa to the table but walked past the chair Eric had pulled out. She went into the kitchen and poured herself some water into a cup. She did not want to allow Eric to think she had been waiting for him to bring her a plate of prison food. It was silent. Neither Sarah nor Eric knew what to say.

Eric turned the TV on and sat down on the sofa. Sarah drank some water, put her cup down hard on the table beside the plate Eric had brought in, went into the bedroom picking her Bible up on the way, closed the bedroom door, and lay on the bed. She opened the Bible to 1 Corinthians chapter 13, <u>The Way of Love</u>. She stopped reading after verse 5. Sarah thought long about verses 4 and 5.

Love suffers long (in the notes it said Love is patient)…
Love is kind…
Love does not dishonor others…
Love is not self-seeking…
Love is not easily angered…
Love keeps no record of wrongs…

Sarah thought about God's meaning of Love. She knew God loved her this way. But how could she love so purely? Sarah knew she had done wrong in betraying Daniel's love for her so many years ago in Ethiopia. How could she expect God to give her someone with a good solid love for her now? She prayed for God's forgiveness and for God's help. Sarah felt God's assurance…

Love keeps no record of wrongs!
Sarah looked up from her prayer and read verse 6 & 7:
Love does not delight in evil, but rejoices with the truth.

Love always protects, always trusts, always hopes, always perseveres!
Sarah closed her eyes again and said, "Amen!"

Eric opened the door to the bedroom, came inside, and sat on the edge of the bed by Sarah's feet. He apologized to her and told her that he would make it right. He would tell his parents they were married as soon as he could. He would tell them she was pregnant with their grandchild and they would accept her. Then Sarah understood. She was obviously pregnant; seven months along and definitely showing. Sarah's child was all out front, and with her thin muscular frame, you could tell she wasn't just fat. Eric had not told them she was pregnant at all. Sarah understood Eric's reluctance to show her to his parents in this situation, but why had he created this situation to begin with? Was he ashamed to tell them? Sarah asked Eric... All he could do was say he did not know. But Sarah could see his shame; Eric could not even look at Sarah when he spoke to her. Sarah scooted to the edge of the bed and sat beside Eric. She put his hand on her tight swollen belly. Sarah told Eric their love for each other and their love for their baby would be enough to get them through this. Eric agreed. They looked in each other's eyes. Sarah could see that Eric did not believe it. But Eric assured Sarah he would tell his parents about their marriage and the baby at dinner that night. Eric also apologized for his drinking the past two days and promised he would not drink again. Sarah remembered what she had just read a few minutes before... "(Love) always trusts..." but somehow, she found it difficult when she looked in Eric's eyes.

Eric stayed with Sarah the rest of that day and night only leaving on a few brief trips to the main house to get food for them to eat. Eric spent most of the day watching television while Sarah watched a bit with him, off and on, but mostly read her Bible in the bedroom.

The next morning, Eric took Sarah to a grocery market to buy food for Sarah to prepare for them in their small guesthouse. Sarah was glad to get out of the small house and considered this a good sign that Eric intended to spend more time with her. She actually enjoyed shopping with him as his attitude seemed to be more free and light. Eric joked with Sarah and made her laugh as they shopped.

Eric stayed home with Sarah most of the rest of that week. Sarah cooked for them. They ate and watched television together. There wasn't very much conversation except about the weather or commenting on news stories. Several times during the day, Sarah would leave Eric alone as he watched TV to go to the bedroom and read her Bible and pray. Most evenings, Eric would go the main house to spend an hour or two with his parents. Sarah would pray that Eric would be brave enough to tell them about his wife and their baby. She would ask Eric when he returned only to be disappointed with his saying she needed to be patient and he would tell them when the time was right. The only real positive interaction time between Sarah and Eric would be when Sarah would feel the baby move and she would let Eric feel her belly.

One day during the middle of their second week in South Africa, Eric's escape from the guesthouse lasted more than a couple hours. He left around 6 P.M. as he normally did, but did not return to Sarah until just before sunrise the next morning. He came in and collapsed on the bed beside Sarah, smelling of alcohol. After she was sure Eric was asleep, Sarah eased out of sheets and went to her knees beside the bed. She thanked God for bringing her husband home safe; she prayed for God to give her strength in faith and forgiveness toward Eric for his weaknesses. She knew God would see her through this difficult time with her husband and strengthen her family. She praised God for all He had done for her and continued to do for her; for keeping her and her baby healthy and safe. Sarah emptied her thoughts to let God speak to her: "Be still and know that I am God!" Amen!

The next day, after Eric woke up, Sarah didn't say anything to Eric about his night out. She let him sleep late as she went to the other room and found a Christian program to watch on TV, it was good to watch something other than the usual sports or violent movies Eric watched. Eric awoke just before noon, and Sarah fixed them sandwiches for lunch. Neither spoke about the previous night. Eric changed the channel on the television to a professional wrestling match, and Sarah went to the bedroom to read her Bible.

Eric started going out for the nights after that, usually two or three times a week. Eric didn't offer to tell Sarah where he was going or where he had been; Sarah didn't ask. Sarah also didn't ask Eric why he was breaking his promise and had stopped asking him when he was going to tell his parents about their marriage and the baby.

Eric eventually did tell his parents about being married to Sarah. One evening after about a month, when Sarah was just over eight months pregnant, Eric came back to the guesthouse after just being gone for about thirty minutes. He took Sarah by the hand and told her to come with him. He took her into the main house. Yes, it was Sarah's first time inside the main house. It had a pleasant aroma, floral, sweet, but not over powering; it was dimly lit, but comfortable; the decorations were dark wood, with dark reds and blues in the curtains and upholstery. Sarah felt a bit uncomfortable as they walked through a long hallway with hunted animal head trophies hung high and long guns mounted below them.

Eric took Sarah into a large room with two sofas, a large sturdy center coffee table, and overstuffed rocking chair, and two small wooden chairs with animal carvings in their backrest. There was a bar with barstools on one side of the room and a large screen television on the other side. Eric's mother and father were sitting on one of the sofas. Eric's father stood up as Eric and Sarah entered the room.

Eric said, "Mom, Dad, this is Sarah, my wife." Like he had rehearsed it and was so proud to be able to finally say it out loud. Sarah didn't know whether to feel proud that her husband had finally found the courage to announce his marriage to his parents or ashamed and embarrassed that it took him so long, about three months since they had been married and over a month since they had been living in his parents' guest house. But Eric's Mom and Dad came to Sarah with smiles on their faces. Eric's Dad told Sarah she was welcome to the family. She saw their eyes glued to her pregnant belly. Dad shook her hand, and Mom immediately reached for Sarah's belly. Sarah was a little uncomfortable, but she felt their enthusiasm for the pregnancy and their joy was contagious. The feeling of togetherness washed her doubts and fears away.

They invited Sarah to sit on the sofa with them as they maneuvered Sarah to sit between them. Eric sat on the edge of the heavy coffee table across from the three of them. Mom and Dad apologized for not knowing she was pregnant and asked her so many questions about how she felt, how far along in the pregnancy she was, if the baby was healthy, when she had last seen a doctor, how active the baby was… Sarah was so thankful they were so receptive to the baby. Eric sat across from them with his big childish smile and blushing. Sarah basked in the moment. Praise God! All is well!

After talking with Eric's parents on the sofa for about thirty minutes, Eric's mother, Constance, took Sarah by the hands and led her to the dining room where they all sat at the table to eat. Constance and Eric went to the kitchen and brought in the food. Dinner was nice. The food and the conversation were appetizing. When dinner was finished, Constance asked Eric to help her clear the table, and Eric's father, Paul, escorted Sarah to the door. Paul walked Sarah to the guesthouse door and told her he was glad to have finally met her; he hoped she and Eric would be happy together and raise the baby in a good Christian home. Paul put his large hand on Sarah's slight but strong shoulder and told her she was welcome. He hoped Sarah and Eric would have dinner with Constance and him every evening.

Sarah went into the guesthouse alone and immediately went to the bedroom and prayed. She thanked God for finally meeting Eric's parents and for their welcoming attitude towards the baby. Although dinner and the conversation had seemed warm enough, she still felt a bit of a chill from Constance and Paul. Perhaps it was just too soon to expect a full welcome for her into the family... perhaps the coolness would fade. For now, though, Sarah knew God was working in her life and everything would be good.

Eric came in about thirty minutes later. Sarah was reading her Bible. He told her that he had been washing dishes and his parents were happy about the baby. They were actually excited to be grandparents.

Sarah and Eric began eating with Constance and Paul every evening. It was nice. Sarah actually went over to the main house early a couple nights to help Constance cook while Eric sat the table and watched television with Paul. Sarah offered to help clear the table and wash dishes every night, but Constance refused to allow her... Constance would tell Sarah she needed to relax and take care of the ("our") baby.

Around noon, two days after the first dinner together, Constance knocked on the door of the guesthouse. Sarah answered the door as Eric was watching television. Constance said that she had arranged for a doctor's appointment for Sarah for a check-up of the baby. Paul was already in the car and they all went to the doctor's office together.

Constance went into the examination room with Sarah as the men sat in the waiting room watching television. The nurse did an ultrasound on Sarah, and Sarah was so amazed to see the image of her child. Constance and Sarah were both so excited to see the child moving and to hear the baby's heartbeat. The doctor came in and felt around Sarah's belly, listened to her heart and the baby's heartbeat. He said everything was good; the baby and Sarah were both very healthy and the baby would be coming soon. Everyone was so elated. Paul drove to a shopping plaza and they all had ice cream. Constance was so happy at dinner that evening. She talked and talked about seeing the baby's image in the ultrasound and how active and healthy the baby was.

Two weeks later, Sarah felt uncomfortable during the day. She had a headache and felt weak, perhaps just tired. During dinner that evening, she started to feel cramps in her belly. The baby became very active and was kicking harder than she had ever felt before. When Sarah scooted back from the table and put her head between her legs trying to relieve the cramp, Constance told Paul to get the car keys. Constance called the doctor, and Eric helped Sarah to the car. Paul drove them all to the hospital. A nurse and an orderly were waiting for Sarah with a hospital gurney when they arrived. The orderly helped Sarah onto the gurney and wheeled her to an examination room while the nurse checked Sarah's pulse. The nurse said Sarah's heart was beating a bit fast, but she seemed to be ok. The nurse put the lubricant on Sarah's belly and began the ultrasound. The baby's heart was beating fast, too. The doctor arrived after a while. Sarah remembers it was difficult to judge time; everything was going fast. The doctor examined Sarah and told her the baby was ready to come. The nurse told Sarah to remove her clothes and put on a hospital gown. After Sarah changed clothes, the nurse prepared Sarah for delivery.

Constance and Eric came into the room as Sarah lay in the hospital bed, in her thin gown, with her knees high up in the air and her feet in the stir-ups. The doctor rolled up a chair alongside Sarah after washing his hands and putting on his gloves. He re-examined Sarah and said the baby was coming.

Eric was sweating severely and his face was flushed. He shook and grabbed a surgical table which slid under his weight. Eric fell to the floor. The doctor and the nurse didn't seem to notice, but Constance asked if he was alright. Eric said he was ok, but he thought he needed to wait outside, and Eric left the room.

Sarah closed her eyes and prayed. Sarah thanked God for all the miracles in her life. Sarah could hear God telling her she was safe and in a good place. Sarah reminded God that her baby was dedicated to God, like Hannah dedicated Samuel. Sarah felt pressure. The cramps were strong. But she felt at rest and knew God was in control. Sarah felt the nurse squeeze her hand and she heard the doctor tell her to push on the next contraction. The cramp came and Sarah pushed. It seemed to last so long, but things were moving faster and faster. The doctor told her to push again. Sarah felt the contraction and she pushed. This one did not last so long and she felt the sharp pressure between her legs. The doctor told her, "One more time, Sarah! Push!"

Sarah felt the contraction again and she pushed. A quick hard push and she felt it was over. Sarah could hear Constance yell, "Hallelujah!"

CHAPTER 18

CHRISTIAN

The doctor yelled, "It's a boy!"

Sarah, relieved but so excited, yelled, "Praise God!"

Sarah says now that she remembers the cramps and pushing but she doesn't remember it actually hurting her. She mostly just remembers the excitement and how close she felt to God.

The doctor handed the baby to the nurse. The nurse cleaned the baby off as the doctor told Sarah to push one final time. Sarah pushed as the remains were released from her womb and the doctor freed the baby from his ties. The nurse handed the baby to Sarah. Sarah looked down at the newborn gift from God and praised God with every bit of her soul. The baby boy was perfect. The doctor told Sarah, "Congratulations!" just as Eric came back into the room.

Eric shouted "A boy! Hell, yeah!" Constance was so shocked; she turned and slapped her son. "Your son was just born; there is no need for talk like that, Eric! We will Praise God here and now for your son!"

Eric said, "Yes, Momma, I am just excited!"

Constance told him she understood and apologized to Eric for slapping him. She also apologized to the doctor for both hers and her son's behavior. She thanked the doctor and the nurse. And then bent over Sarah to look at the baby. Sarah looked up at Constance and said, "He is perfect! A perfect gift from God!"

Constance agreed, "Yes, he is! Praise God!"

The doctor and the nurse left the room. A few minutes later, the nurse returned with a bassinette and forms for Sarah to fill out. The nurse took the baby from Sarah and placed him in the bassinette. She said that she would fully examine the baby while Sarah filled out the papers. Sarah asked Eric to help her fill out the papers, but Constance said he was too excited and she would help Sarah fill them out. Constance took the papers. Constance immediately filled out what she knew and asked Sarah the questions from the forms she didn't know, mostly the questions about Sarah. When they got to the box for the baby's name, Sarah said, immediately without hesitation, "Christian!"

June 2014. Sarah and Eric had a healthy son, Christian. Constance and Paul had a beautiful grandson, Christian. Sarah praised God for her precious gift from God, Christian.

Constance doted on Christian excessively for the two-day stay in the hospital. The nurses even had to ask Constance to leave the room a few times while Sarah fed Christian because Constance would not let the baby rest in Sarah's arms. During these days in the hospital, Constance took good care of Sarah, too. She brought Sarah extra food to eat and juice to drink. When the nurses would ask her to leave the room for nursing and mother bonding time, Constance would always cover Christian and Sarah up with an extra blanket.

Paul would come into the room every couple of hours to check on Constance, Christian, and Sarah. Sometimes he would bring them chicken strips from the café. But Sarah thought it was strange that no one mentioned Eric. Eric was not there since just after the delivery. Sarah asked about him once or twice, and Constance just said Eric had been busy and he would probably be by to check on them later. But he never came.

After Sarah and Christian were released from the hospital, Sarah's pre-baby life in South Africa changed. Paul drove Sarah, Constance, and Christian home, and Eric met them at the front of the house, standing in the front doorway. Eric came down to the car and they all made their way to the front door. Paul led the way, caring the baby's bassinette filled with diapers and other baby supplies. Next, Constance carried Christian. Coming from the car last was Eric and Sarah. Sarah was strong enough to walk on her own, but Eric, acting like the caring husband, assisted her from the car, up the front porch stairs, and into the house.

Constance told Sarah to follow her. They went down a long dark hallway. Constance stopped Sarah when they came to a closed door. Constance, still holding Baby Christian, told Sarah to go into the room. Sarah opened the door to a dark room and turned on the light. Sarah was surprised to see the room was decorated with baby trimmings, pastel blues and greens, a large mobile of small stuffed animals hung from the ceiling light in the center of the room giving them an alternating eerie glow and shadow, a dresser, a single bed, two wooden rocking chairs, and a crib.

Constance followed Sarah into the room and placed Christian into the crib. Constance announced that this is the baby's room. She continued saying, almost as an afterthought, that Sarah could stay here too until she healed from the delivery or even until Christian was able to sleep alone. Of course, Sarah understood from the single bed that Eric would be expected to sleep elsewhere. Paul placed the bassinette down at the foot of the crib. He passed by the side of the crib, bent over, and gave Christian a kiss on the cheek on his way out of the room. Eric was standing at the doorway and moved to the side, closer to Sarah, as Paul squeezed past him to exit. Sarah looked at Eric as he moved closer to her. Her look was obviously questioning the new living arrangements. Eric shrugged with a look of understanding but a seemingly reluctant agreement.

Constance also kissed Christian on the cheek, covered him with a baby blanket, tucked him in, kissed him again, and left the room. Eric shut the door after his mother had left and he observed that she was clear of the hallway. When the door was shut, Sarah, still watching her voice volume, asked Eric where would he be sleeping and why they had to be apart. She was excited to be included in the house, but wanted to be with her husband as a family should be. Eric told her that he still had his bedroom in the house, just down the hall from the baby's room, but his mother would prefer him to stay in the guesthouse most nights. It seemed so strange to Sarah. She just wanted to be a family.

Eric showed Sarah the drawers in the dresser that he had moved all her clothes into while she was in the hospital. He also showed her where the stocks of baby supplies were. He seemed proud of how he had arranged everything. But Sarah stopped him as he was moving around the room and asked him why they couldn't be together? Eric explained that his mother didn't want them sleeping together in the house. But, in a week or two, they could be back out in the guesthouse together. He also told her he thought he had a line on a good job and they would be able to rent their own place soon. Eric kissed Sarah on the cheek, went to the crib and kissed Christian, then left the room. Sarah sat on the edge of the bed, trying not to cry. She then went to the crib. Sarah balanced her elbows on the side of the crib, put her hands together over

Baby Christian, and prayed. Sarah praised God for her son. She told God she would do all she could to keep Christian dedicated to God. She thanked God for all the times He had protected her and provided for her. She thanked God for the care given to her and Christian at the hospital. Sarah asked God to continue to watch over her and her family and to keep them together and happy in Christ. Amen!

Sarah and Christian stayed in the main house for about two months. It was a good time for Sarah: She had her baby with her, Christian and she were healthy, and Paul and Constance were good and friendly to her. Constance would bring Sarah a good full breakfast to the baby room early every morning. Constance would come into the room with the breakfast on a tray, usually as Sarah was sitting in the chair beside the crib nursing Christian. Constance would sit in the other rocking chair, holding the tray and patiently wait until Christian finished his breakfast. After Sarah finished Christian's morning feeding, they would exchange the breakfast try for Christian. Sarah would eat the breakfast while Constance held her precious grandson. Constance would hold Christian as he napped; she would read to him and play with his fingers and toes while he was awake. Everything revolved around Christian.

Sarah would usually take the tray to the kitchen, leaving Constance holding Christian. After a while of holding Christian, while he was sleeping, Constance would lay him in the crib and sing softly to him. Christian hardly ever cried, mostly only when he was hungry. Sarah would wash the breakfast dishes and go into the main room to watch television. If Paul was already watching TV, she would sit on the sofa and watch whatever he was watching with him. Paul hardly ever spoke to Sarah other than to quickly ask her how Christian was doing. If Paul were not there, she would watch the Christian programming channel, singing praises and delivering powerful spiritual messages.

Sometimes Sarah would go out back to the guesthouse and check to see if Eric were there. He was hardly ever there. Sarah actually very rarely saw Eric. He hardly ever even came in to see Christian. Sarah assumed that most days, Eric was out looking for a job. Sarah also knew that he was spending most evenings out drinking with his friends. Sarah promised herself that she would not bring that up to him… It was a demon he would have to deal with. She did hear Eric come into the house some nights and argue with his mother, but as soon as his father came into the room, Eric would leave. It did worry Sarah at times, that when they would be on their own, if he was still drinking like he had been since they have been in South Africa, would he shout at her and Christian? Sometimes Sarah frightened herself with thoughts of Eric developing violent behavior towards her. She consoled herself that God was with her and Christian, always.

On the rare occasions when Sarah did see Eric, he would ask how she and Christian were doing and tell Sarah he was still looking for a job. Eric would assure her he would get a good job soon. Eric also told Sarah that once Christian was weaned, able to take bottled milk, Sarah could move back into the guesthouse and they would be closer again. He further told Sarah she could get a job, Mom would take care of Christian while she was at work, and they would save for their own place. Otherwise, Eric was quiet and cold towards Sarah and even colder towards Christian. Sarah didn't understand why Eric was so different now, so very distant. Perhaps he had been spoiled as the only child and resented all the attention Christian was receiving from Sarah and Eric's mother. Sarah prayed about Eric often and resolved that she would try to show him more attention, but the opportunities were seldom and she found herself actually emotionally distancing herself more and more from the man she had taken to love.

Constance bought Sarah a breast pump when Christian was three weeks old, so Sarah could bottle his milk. Constance said it was for Sarah so she could relax more and have some free time away from Christian. It was obvious, however, that Constance wanted to use this opportunity so she could feed Christian herself and hold him more. But Sarah did appreciate the time, a little more time to sleep at night, a little more time to walk around the house during the day and even watch an entire Church service on television without having to run to feed Christian when he cried. Sarah did acknowledge the help Constance gave her, changing Christian's diapers, and now feeding him during the day. And Christian was beginning to sleep longer at night now, and that helped Sarah, too.

Sometimes Sarah would go outside and go for long walks admiring the beauty and sounds of God's creation. The sunlight felt good on her skin, warm and welcome. Sarah would praise God out loud as she walked, thanking God for all his wonders, both of the Earth and in her life; for the sunlight, for the soft cool breeze on her skin, for the flowers and the trees; and for God's protection of her; and mostly, she thanked God for her son.

When Christian was two months old, Sarah told Constance that she was missing Eric so much and that Christian needed to spend more time with his father. She emphasized to Constance that she appreciated all that she and Paul had done and continued to do for her and Christian, but she thought it was time to move back to the guesthouse with Eric.

Constance began crying, but said she understood. She told Sarah that Christian and Sarah would always be welcome in the main house and the room would stay as it is. She said she would send Paul to buy another crib for the guesthouse and asked Sarah to stay until the crib in the guesthouse was ready. Sarah agreed.

Paul did buy a new crib for the guesthouse three days later. He set it up in the main room of the guesthouse as there was not sufficient room in the bedroom. Sarah moved her clothes back to the guesthouse. She took some of Christian's clothes, but Constance asked her to leave some in the baby room, too. Constance cried as Sarah moved back and forth moving clothing and baby supplies, especially on Sarah's last walk back to the guesthouse carrying Christian to his new crib. It was like they were moving a thousand miles instead of just across the courtyard.

Life was generally good for Sarah in the guesthouse. She had everything she needed. Sarah would usually cook her own breakfast but would go over to the main house and eat lunch with Constance. Constance was always so happy to see Christian and welcomed Sarah at every opportunity. Sometimes Paul would eat with them too, when he was home.

Eric was very seldom around during the day. Well, Eric was very seldom home at all, even spending many nights out drinking and staying with his friends. Sometimes he would come home very late, even early the next morning, sometimes not coming home for two or three days in a row.

Sarah and Eric hardly spoke at all after Christian was born. Sometimes Sarah tried to talk to him about their future, but Eric would always get angry and leave. Sarah thought that somehow, when she was pregnant, it gave Eric hope of a good family life, but after Christian was actually born, Eric gave up. Sarah knew Eric was disappointed in himself for losing his job with the United Nations in Uganda, and not getting a job immediately after arriving back in South Africa... She wasn't even sure Eric was looking anymore. And she knew that Paul, his father, was always putting Eric down for not working and for drinking too much. When Eric was home in the evening, he would just watch television. The nights Eric was home, he would sleep in the bed with Sarah, but they never touched each other. Sometimes, when Eric would come home drunk and try to get close to Sarah in the bed, she would go sleep on sofa. Sometimes, when Eric would be yelling and seeming to get violent, Sarah would take Christian to the main house and sleep in the baby room.

Time went by. Christian grew. Constance was the only person, other than Christian, that Sarah really talked to. Constance was always around. Sarah knew it was just so Constance could be close to Christian, but that was ok. Sometimes it was good to have a woman to talk to, even if was just mostly talking about Christian.

Some days, Constance would come to the guesthouse early in the morning and take Christian to the main house. On these occasions, Sarah would go outside and take long walks down the country road. Days, and weeks, and months went by. Life was a bit lonely for Sarah, but she praised God for all God had done in her life, for her son, and for their health. Christian grew and God was Good. Praise God!

When Christian was six months old, Sarah asked Paul to take her into the small towns not far from their house to look for a job. After a week, Sarah finally found a job working at a roadside market selling honey and souvenirs to travelers. She couldn't work in South Africa officially, because she was still on a visitor's visa, so she was paid with just a percentage of the earnings. She didn't need the money, as her and Christian's needs were met. They had food and a safe place to live. Sarah just needed to get out and interface with other people. Sarah kept what money she earned in a jar in the small kitchen of the guesthouse, but she soon found that Eric was taking most of it. It didn't matter. God provided all she and Christian needed. Time passed… months passed. Christian grew. Sarah and Christian stayed healthy. Sarah missed Christian during the long days working, but that just made the joy of seeing him when she got home that much better. God was Good.

Eventually, Paul helped Sarah apply and obtain a work visa so she could apply for better jobs. After approximately a year, Sarah got a job at a clothing shop in one of the nearby small towns. She enjoyed being out of the house and meeting new people. Sarah was overjoyed to see Christian at the end of each day. Christian would light up and be so happy to see his mother every evening when she arrived home. He was a very happy baby anyway. Sarah going out and working all day was sweet for Constance too.

Constance loved Christian so very much and she relished taking care of her grandchild every day. She would be knocking on the door to the guesthouse every morning, as early as she could, to take Christian to the main house. Sarah would follow and eat breakfast before Paul drove her to work. Constance always had activities planned for Christian, building blocks, finger painting, watching preschool cartoons on the television. Sometimes Constance's sister, Charity, would come and take Constance and Christian to her house where she had a swimming pool.

Months passed. Christian was walking by nine months. Christian turned one year old with a huge birthday party. Everyone in both Constance and Paul's families came to celebrate. Christian was growing so fast now and a pleasure to everyone in the family. Christian turned two years old. Another big family party. Christian began talking and made everyone he talked to laugh. Christian turned three, then four, delighting Constance, Paul, and everyone, family and friends, that visited. Constance and Paul would tell Sarah of how everything Christian did amazed and delighted everyone. But Sarah only got to spend an hour or two with her son each evening. And Christian's father hardly ever enjoyed the blessings of his son at all.

Since Sarah had started working, and Christian was spending more time with Constance, Sarah felt more alone and ostracized than ever. Sarah was grateful to have her job and to be interacting with people there, but at home she was shut off. Eric almost never talked to her. He still did not have a job and in his self-disappointment, Eric continued to spend most days and evenings away at friend's houses drinking and coming home drunk, late at night, or not at all. Constance only talked to Sarah when she was receiving Christian in the morning or when Sarah would pick Christian up in the evening, and even then just a little small talk about what Christian had done during the day. Paul only talked to Sarah in courtesy gestures. Sometimes Paul would bring up an oddity of the weather or a bit of news on the ride to Sarah's work or the drive home. Sarah rejoiced as Christian started to talk more and he actually engaged in conversation with Mommy in the evenings before going to bed. Even though they only shared this precious little time together in the evenings, she could tell Christian loved her very much. Sarah, however, still felt like she was being pushed away from Christian. Christian would talk about what he and Nana had done together all day. Sarah found herself feeling like an outsider in her own son's life.

CHAPTER 19
FINDING A WAY THROUGH THE DARKNESS

This part of Sarah and Christian's relationships and life began to change when Sarah decided and convinced Constance it was time for Christian to go to pre-school. He was four and needed to get used to school and socialize with other children before beginning kindergarten when he turned 5 years old.

Paul took Christian and Sarah to get Christian's national Identification Card and a South African Passport so he could be registered at pre-school. The passport was not required, but it was done at the same facility as the national ID and was recommended to be done at the same time. Sarah had taken off work that day so they could do what they needed to do to get Christian registered and in pre-school. Paul began taking Christian to pre-school on the way to drop Sarah off at her work. Christian would only spend half the day at pre-school, so Constance still had the afternoons with her precious grandson. But at least Christian had more news to tell Sarah in the evenings other than about him and Nana. Christian would be so excited in the evenings to tell Mommy all about his new friends at school and all the good school work he had done.

The little time Eric was at home with Sarah, he was rude and argumentative with her. Eric became increasingly violent and abusive to Sarah, yet still merely vocal and psychological... not physical. It seemed to Sarah that Eric was bullying her, but did not seem to have the courage to do anything physical to her for fear of his parents. Sarah felt sorry for Eric as he was obviously afraid of his parents and ashamed of his behavior and their lack of pride in him. But Eric lacked the fortitude to change anything. He made promises many times to Sarah that things would get better. But she doubted they would. All she could do was pray that God would make a change.

On Christian's 5th birthday, Constance and Paul had a huge family birthday party for him. This time they had the party at Aunt Charity's house so Christian could swim in the pool. Aunt Charity also had horses. Christian loved swimming and horseback riding so much. He was so proud of himself for being able to do both. Of course they had the party while Sarah worked. Christian was so excited to tell Mommy about the great day swimming and horseback riding.

Eric actually came home early that evening, just as Christian was retelling his exciting day to Sarah. Eric was drunk and exploded, shouting how he could not even enjoy his wife or his son. Eric began throwing things. Sarah grabbed Christian and left the guesthouse, exiting just as a large glass water pitcher crashed against the door. Sarah took Christian into the main house and they slept in the baby room that night. Constance came, knocked on the door, and asked why they had come to the room so late and if Christian was ok. Sarah told Constance through the door that Christian was ok… just that Eric had come in late, was loud, and had woke Christian. She said she wanted to bring Christian to the room to be quiet so Christian could go back to sleep. Constance agreed and went back to bed. Sarah cried and prayed. She was afraid that Constance would defend Eric and try to take Christian away from her. Sarah praised God for always being with her and asked that God would continue to be with her, give her wisdom, and give her a way out. After praying, Sarah was convinced that she would have to leave the next day.

Very early the next morning, before the sun arose, Sarah woke Christian up and took him to the guesthouse. Eric was sleeping hard. She put as much of hers and Christian's clothes and supplies in bags. Sarah let Christian carry a plastic bag of clothes and she grabbed the others. Sarah held Christian's hand and asked him to be quiet as they went out the door of the guesthouse, around the main house, to the road. The sun was just coming up providing sufficient light for them to see as they walked down the quiet road. There was a bright yellow-orange light stretching across the horizon. Sarah knew God was shining a light on their path. Soon a car came along and asked if they needed a ride. Sarah accepted and they went to the clothing shop where Sarah worked.

Sarah explained to her boss the difficult situation she was in. The owner of the clothing store was Lebanese and understood how difficult it was to be a foreigner in South Africa. He told Sarah that she and Christian could stay at his house with him and his wife until she found another place to stay. He and his wife were Lebanese Christians. They had experienced discrimination in South Africa and understood how Sarah had been treated. The Lebanese Maronite Christians practiced similarly to the Ethiopian Orthodox that Sarah was used to.

Sarah's boss, Barnaba, took Sarah to his house and introduced her and Christian to his wife, Azara. Barnaba and Azara got them settled in the guest room. Sarah was not sure if she could handle talking to Paul, as she was confident he would come to the store to look for her, as he dropped her off there for work every day. Sarah did not feel confident or strong enough for the confrontation yet. Paul might even bring Eric with him and Sarah knew she would not be able to handle seeing Eric. She spent the day praying and playing with Christian and going over his school work with him. Azara was very empathetic and comforting to Sarah. Azara fixed them a good lunch and joined in with Sarah helping Christian with his spelling and math studies.

Barnaba returned home late in the afternoon and told Sarah that Paul had come by the store (alone) to ask about Sarah. Barnaba had told Paul that Sarah was safe. He told him what Sarah had told him about the night before and that Sarah had been very frightened. She was staying with a friend and would be taking a few days off from work, but she would call Eric soon. Barnaba reported to Sarah that Paul had told him Eric had left the house and said he would not be back. Paul said Sarah was welcome to come back anytime. Paul left Barnaba after telling him that Constance and Paul missed Christian and Sarah so much already and they only wanted the best for them.

Sarah was sure that Constance and Paul missed and loved Christian very much, but was not sure that Constance would protect Sarah from Eric. Sarah could imagine that Eric and his parents had such a huge fight over Sarah taking Christian away. She was sure that Eric was defensive and argumentative and probably ended up by pretending like he did not even care. She could see in her mind Constance yelling at Eric for pushing her precious grandson away, Eric yelling back, and Paul telling Eric to leave. It must have been very dramatic and loud.

Sarah sat on the sofa with Azara as Barnaba told her of Paul's visit. Sarah began to cry as she thought of the drama and how things had become so tragic for Christian. Azara took Sarah into her arms and attempted to comfort her. Sarah was sure she did the right thing in leaving to protect Christian and herself, but... perhaps... could she have stayed a bit longer and tried harder to make it work? Sarah was confused. Azara told Sarah her leaving when she did was the best thing for Christian. A child should not see his father acting violent. Sarah agreed and her mind started to clear.

Sarah left Azara and went to the guest bedroom where her and Christian's things were. Sarah knelt by the bed and prayed. She praised God for their safety, for God keeping her and her son in His Mighty Hands; she thanked God for Barnaba and Azara; and she prayed for continued help, strength, and guidance.

Sarah stayed at Barnaba's home, away from work, for a couple days, but then she went back to work. Barnaba and Azara made Sarah feel welcome in their home. Azara loved being with children and did not have any of her own, so she enjoyed spending the days with Christian. She bought him school books and home-schooled him while Sarah went to work.

Sarah was still afraid of Paul or Eric coming to her work, but they didn't come, at least not for a while. Sarah called Eric after the first week of her being gone passed, but he said he did not want to talk to her and their conversation ended quick with him hanging up. Paul and Constance came to the shop after about two weeks. They had brought some new clothes and school books for Christian and invited Sarah to bring Christian to come to the house for lunch or dinner sometime. Sarah said she would call them soon to arrange a visit. Sarah did call them later in the week and she and Christian did go to lunch there that Saturday, and most Saturdays after that. Soon, Constance had arranged with Sarah to pick-up and keep Christian every other weekend. Eric, however, as far as Sarah knew, was still not around. Constance and Paul were appreciative of Sarah allowing them to have Christian on the weekends they agreed upon and they were good about bringing him back early on those Sunday evenings. Constance reminded Sarah often, but not harassingly, that Sarah and Christian were welcome to move back to the house. Sarah would show appreciation for the invitations but always declined.

CHAPTER 20
MORNING LIGHT RETURNING

It was a good arrangement for Sarah, working for Barnaba at the clothing store, living with Barnaba and Azara, Azara home-schooling Christian, and Christian visiting Constance and Paul every other weekend. But, after a couple months, Eric began coming by the clothing store harassing and even yelling at Sarah. He claimed he wanted his family back, but often Sarah could tell he had been drinking, smelling the liquor on his breath and sensing his over-aggressiveness. Usually Barnaba would have to tell Eric to leave, even threatening to call the police before Eric would leave. Eric would call Sarah at night and tell her he had a job and give her hope that her family life might be reconnected, only for Sarah to find out a few days later that he had lost his job, or sometimes that he had lied about even having a new job.

Sarah decided to move further away from Eric, Constance, and Paul about six months after leaving their house. Barnaba had a close friend and fellow Lebanese Maronite Christian that owned a computer tech store in Pretoria, the Executive Government Capital of South Africa. Barnaba's friend, Elias, and his wife Zaina had three young children, a large house, and were willing to accept Sarah and Christian into their home. Sarah would work at Elias's store and Christian could go to a nearby school. Sarah prayed for God's guidance that this was the right decision. She felt God leading her to move. Elias, Zaina, and their children came to visit Barnaba and Azara. Elias and Zaina met Sarah and they all had a good conversation over dinner. The children played with Christian and they all got along well. Elias drove his family, with the new additions of Sarah and Christian, back to their home in Pretoria. A couple weeks later, Sarah and Christian spent Christmas with their new family.

2020 saw new horizons in Sarah's life. Sarah and Christian stayed with Zaina and Elias for a few months. They all became best of friends and were like family. In April, as summer in Pretoria began to come to an end, Elias and Barnaba helped Sarah get her own apartment so she and Christian could live on their own. Sarah continued to work for Elias at the computer store. The store did very well, and Elias appreciated Sarah's hard work. Christian did well in school. Zaina picked him up with her own children after school and watched him until Sarah came after work to take him to their own apartment.

Elias helped Sarah find a lawyer. Sarah filed for divorce from Eric. At first the courts were reluctant to proceed with the case, as Sarah was not an actual South African citizen. They assigned mediators and social workers to the case. Eric (probably with the pushing of his mother and father) filed counter-suits saying Sarah was an unfit mother. However, as time passed, time after time:

- Eric missing mediation sessions;
- Social case workers reporting on Eric's several drunken episodes;
- Police reports detailing Eric's disorderly conduct;
- Police reports on Eric breaching the court ordered protection orders when Eric would go to Sarah's drunk during unscheduled times and become verbally abusive;
- Eric physically assaulted and injured a deliveryman serving a trial date court order;
- Eric's personal behavior during mediation sessions and in the courtroom;

The court finally awarded Sarah full custody of Christian with every other weekend visitation for Constance and Paul. Eric's visits were ordered to be monthly with court ordered social worker supervision, but Eric never came to visit. Sarah has actually never seen Eric since the divorce was officially issued.

The visits with Christian's grandparents go well. Constance and Paul have very little to say to Sarah when they pick Christian up and drop him off, but they take good care of Christian and have fun with him. Sometimes they take Christian to their home; sometimes to Constance's sister's home so Christian can swim and ride the horses; sometimes they take him to a fair or other special event. Christian always talks so much about all the good things he does when he is with them. But he loves his mother so much and is always so happy to be back with her.

It is a good, stable life now. Sarah would have preferred for a life with her husband and father of her child present in their lives, but she is thankful that God has brought her through all the trials in her life. Sarah prays every morning, every night, and many times during each day, thanking and praising God for His protection over her life. She recounts all the blessings in her life and knows that God is with her. God has always been with her. God is with her now. God has given her and her son a good life now and she knows God will always be with her.

- Sarah is independent, relying only on God and the strength he has provided her.
- Sarah's experiences give her assurance that God will always be there for her.
- Sarah has proven she is -
  - ❖ Strong enough to take the pain,
  - ❖ Inflicted, again and again.

Many African women, and many women all over the world, believe they need a man; they depend on a man, a man to provide for them, a man to protect them, a man to make them complete. Sarah proved she only requires God and the strength God gives her; her belief that Christ has saved her soul and that God is always with her. God is her Provider! God is her Protector! God has given her a son and continues to complete her!

Sarah is the absolute epitome of a strong woman of faith and displays the true strength of an African woman!